"He's trying to kill us!" Addy cried.

Shawn ducked down, sending their SUV swerving wildly. He swore, his gaze locked on something in front of them.

A sharp curve with a steep drop-off loomed up ahead. The continued shots coming from behind them cautioned against slowing down.

Shawn gripped the steering wheel tight enough to turn his knuckles white. He tapped the brakes as they rode into the turn at a much-too-fast speed.

The motorcyclist drew even with them and swerved to the right. Metal screamed as the passenger side of the SUV scraped along the road barrier.

"Hang on!" Shawn stomped on the gas.

The motorcycle slammed into the back of their car, sending them spinning. Shawn struggled to regain control of the vehicle.

They slid from the road, the driver's side of the car scraping along the barrier until they made it to the end.

But their SUV couldn't stop...

MISSING AT CHRISTMAS

K.D. RICHARDS

HARLEQUIN
INTRIGUE

To Bryson and Miles.

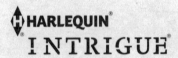

HARLEQUIN®
INTRIGUE®

Recycling programs
for this product may
not exist in your area.

ISBN-13: 978-1-335-55531-1

Missing at Christmas

Copyright © 2021 by Kia Dennis

This edition published by arrangement with Harlequin Books S.A.

For questions and comments about the quality of this book,
please contact us at CustomerService@Harlequin.com.

Harlequin Enterprises ULC
22 Adelaide St. West, 40th Floor
Toronto, Ontario M5H 4E3, Canada
www.Harlequin.com

Printed in U.S.A.

K.D. Richards is a native of the Washington, DC, area, who now lives outside Toronto with her husband and two sons. You can find her at kdrichardsbooks.com.

Books by K.D. Richards

Harlequin Intrigue

West Investigations

Pursuit of the Truth
Missing at Christmas

Visit the Author Profile page at Harlequin.com.

CAST OF CHARACTERS

Shawn West—Co-owner of West Security and Investigation and private investigator.

Adelaide (Addy) Williams—An attorney looking for her younger sister, who has been missing for nearly two weeks.

Cassie Williams—Addy's younger sister; works for Spectrum.

Ryan West—Co-owner of West Security and Investigation, private investigator and Shawn's brother.

Martin Raupp—Owner of Spectrum Securities.

Ben Konstam—Cassie's boyfriend.

Laurence Raupp—VP of Spectrum Securities.

Chapter One

Adelaide "Addy" Williams's feet ached, and a headache throbbed behind her temples as she pulled the restaurant door open. The bells above the door jangled, drawing the attention of the middle-aged man behind the host podium. The smell of fried onions and beef slapped her in the face as she stepped toward the man.

He gave a tight smile, probably annoyed to have a customer come in less than an hour from closing time. "Dining in or taking out?"

"Neither." Addy pulled the photograph of her sister from the oversize purse she carried. The bottom edges were creased from having been taken in and out of the purse all day, but Cassie's effervescent smile remained unblemished. "I'm looking for my sister." Addy thrust the photo at the man. "Have you seen her?"

The man flicked a glance at the photo then back to Addy. "No."

Addy fought back the annoyance swelling in

her chest. She'd gotten the same reaction from at least half the people she'd shown Cassie's picture to over the last two days. Indifference or outright irritation was the most common reaction from people when she explained her nineteen-year-old sister was missing. She couldn't help but wonder if she'd have gotten the same reaction if Cassie had blue eyes and blond hair instead of caramel skin and coarse coils.

"Please, look again," she said, thrusting Cassie's photo closer to the man.

He sighed, but pulled a pair of glasses from the pocket of his suit jacket and slipped them on before taking the photo from Addy. A lock of dark brown hair fell over his forehead as his studied the picture. After a moment he said, "I'm sorry. I've never seen her."

"Are you sure?" Addy pressed, taking the photo back. She'd been in the restaurant earlier that day and had gotten the same response from the young woman behind the podium at the time, but she'd hoped she might have better luck with the evening staff.

The man sighed. "Yes, I'm sure. Now, I'm sorry about your sister, but if you aren't going to order something, I have to ask you to leave."

As if on cue, Addy's stomach rumbled.

The man's dark eyebrows rose, making it clear he'd heard her body's protestations. She'd forgotten to stop for lunch, propelled by the ticking clock metaphorically hanging over her head. Addy knew the statistics. The longer a young woman was missing, the less likely it was that she'd be found alive.

"Kitchen is closing in five minutes, but the dining area is open until nine."

Addy glanced at her watch—8:25 p.m. Living in Manhattan, it was nearly impossible to imagine a restaurant closing up shop so early. But Bentham, New York, was no Manhattan.

"Miss?" the man said.

"I want to order. I'll take it to go."

The man grabbed a plastic-clad menu from the top of the stack on the podium and thrust it into her hands. It listed traditional Mexican fare. She ordered a chicken burrito.

"Have a seat." The man waved vaguely toward the nearest cluster of tables. "Your order will be out momentarily." He dropped the menu back on top of the stack and turned.

"Do you mind showing this photo to the kitchen staff? Please?" Addy added at his frown. "She's my sister." She fought to get the last words out around the sob lodged in her throat. Showing vulnerability in front of a complete stranger was not something a tough-as-nails corporate attorney from Manhattan did.

But if she had to beg this man to help her, she would. She couldn't leave any stone unturned.

The man's eyes finally softened. He took the photo from her hand. "I'll see what I can do."

Addy watched him disappear through swinging doors she assumed led to the kitchen, then fell into one of the chairs at the nearest table to wait for her dinner.

Cassie taking a day or two to return a call hadn't alarmed Addy at first. Cassie was nineteen, adventurous and far more impulsive than Addy had ever been. After the first few missed calls and texts, Addy had expected a call from Cassie recounting a fun-filled last-minute trip to the mountains or someone's vacation house in the Hamptons.

But that call had never come, and Cassie hadn't answered any of Addy's subsequent calls or texts. By the fourth day of silence, Addy had become concerned enough to reach out to Cassie's roommate, Suri. Worry transformed to fear when Suri said Cassie had packed her things and moved out. Addy had resisted the impulse to call Cassie's boss, not wanting to embarrass her sister at her first real job, but at that point, there was no other choice. Over the phone, Ms. Webb, the head of human resources and Cassie's boss, informed Addy that Cassie had resigned from her internship with the company almost a week earlier with no notice.

Cassie had been over the moon to land the internship with Spectrum Industries, a leading computer chip manufacturer in the area. For Cassie, who was headed to MIT to study computer science after finishing this gap year between graduating high school and college, the internship was a dream come true. There was no way Cassie would have quit.

Something was very wrong, yet Addy felt in her bones that Cassie was out there somewhere. Alive.

She'd hoped to be heading back to New York, having found some clue to where Cassie was or at least having convinced the sheriff of the urgency of the situation, but she'd accomplished neither. Which meant she'd have to do the one thing she was hoping to avoid.

Addy pulled out her phone and scrolled through her contacts. She tapped Jarod Cunningham's name and hoped he wouldn't answer.

Her boss picked up on the third ring.

"Addy? Didn't expect to hear from you this evening. Is everything okay with the merger?"

That was Jarod. All business. She had no idea where Jarod currently was, since she'd called him on his cell phone, but it wasn't hard to imagine him in his twenty-second-floor corner office even after eight on a Sunday night.

"Everything is fine with the merger, Jarod. It's Cassie, my sister. You know she's gone missing and I spent the weekend in Bentham looking for her. I'm still here, actually, and I'm going to need to stay a few more days."

She'd avoided requesting time off initially by driving up on Friday after work. Asking the head of the corporate law practice at Covington and Baker for time off was always a fraught endeavor. Despite the firm marketing itself as a place where work-life balance was valued, when it came down to it Covington and Baker, just like every other big New York law firm, expected the balance to come down on the side of work, not life. She had just been assigned to one of the biggest mergers the firm had ever landed, a deal that would make her upcoming partnership vote a given as long as everything went perfectly.

And asking for time off just days before they were scheduled to meet the client wasn't the way she'd envisioned starting things off.

It wasn't what Jarod had envisioned, either.

"You can't be serious," Jarod bellowed. "Now is really not a good time to take a vacation. We need you here."

"It's not a vacation, Jarod. My sister is missing." Addy let out an angry breath. She'd worked hard to prove her value to Jarod, and she resented the insinuation that she was blowing off a major deal to sip mai tais on the beach.

Although Jarod brought in a lot of the merger business, as his right-hand woman, Addy did most of the work. It was a position she was content, if not happy, to be in. It wasn't easy to be a Black woman in a large law firm. She was the only Black associate in the corporate practice, one of three Black female senior associates or partners in the whole of the two-hundred-person New York office.

"Of course, of course, and we all feel for you," Jarod said, his voice lower now but still lacking all hint of sympathy. "But really, isn't this a job for the police?"

She didn't disagree, but the authorities didn't seem to be taking the situation seriously. "The sheriff thinks Cassie will turn up on her own in a few days." He hadn't even wanted to take a missing person report. Luckily, seven years as a corporate attorney had given her a lot of experience convincing obstinate men to listen to her.

"If you can just wait two, maybe three weeks," Jarod continued. "The Browning–Tuffs merger will be done by then. I bet your sister will have turned up by that point as well, and the two of you can take a nice long vacation."

"My sister is the only family I have. I'm not just going to sit around doing nothing while she's missing." She didn't try to hide the iciness in her tone.

"You wouldn't be doing nothing, Addy. You'd be doing your job."

She bit back her reflexive response. He was a talented attorney, but like a lot of powerful men, he was also a major jerk. For maybe the millionth time in the seven years since she'd started working at Covington and Baker, she considered quitting. And like each time before, she pushed the thought away, reminding herself how close she was to finally making partner and getting out from under Jarod's thumb and how many medical bills were still left to pay from her father's illness.

She took a deep breath and let it out slowly. "We don't meet with the client until Thursday. I'm ready for the meeting, and I have my laptop with me, so I can do any last-minute changes from here."

"I don't like it," Jarod said, but his hesitation gave her hope.

"Jarod, you know me. You know I can handle it. And I'll be back no later than Thursday."

Several silent seconds passed.

"Fine." Jarod sighed loudly on the other end of the line. "But nothing can go wrong with this meeting, Addy. This deal is just as important for you as it is for me." He disconnected from the call.

Jarod was not known for his subtlety, but he also wasn't wrong. She knew the stakes.

She had three days to find Cassie.

The doors to the kitchen swung outward, and the man reappeared, a white plastic bag in one hand and Cassie's picture in the other.

Addy slid her phone back into her purse and rose. The pity she saw in the man's face as he drew nearer dashed the hope that had swelled in her chest.

"I showed your sister's picture to everyone who's still here, and no one recognized her. I'm sorry."

Two solid days of showing Cassie's picture everywhere she could think of in Bentham and nothing. No one remembered seeing her.

"Thanks, anyway." She didn't bother trying to muster a smile of thanks. She reached in her purse for her wallet.

"No charge," he said, thrusting her food and Cassie's picture at her. "You take care of yourself."

Addy looked up into the man's now compassion-filled eyes and wiped away the single tear she couldn't stop from falling. "Thank you," she croaked out before turning and fleeing the restaurant before the dam of tears broke.

Silver garlands hung from the streetlamps along with fluttering signs ordering the denizens of Bentham to have a happy holiday. The lamps themselves were spaced too far apart for the weak yellow light they cast off to beat back the dark December night. Five blocks west, cars coasted along one of Bentham's main thoroughfares, but the street in front of Addy was clear and quiet, the surrounding businesses having long since closed for the night.

She'd left the metallic-blue Mustang she'd rented for the two-hour drive from Manhattan to Bentham in the hotel's parking lot. It was easier to canvass the neighborhood on foot. All she had to show for her effort were sore feet.

A footstep sounded as she pocketed her phone. Shooting a glance over her shoulder, she squinted into the darkness but saw no one.

You're just not used to so much quiet, she thought, walking on.

She'd lived in New York City since she was twelve but spent summers on her grandfather's ranch in Texas. She'd loved the ranch almost as much as she loved the city, but New York wasn't called the city that never slept for nothing. There was always something to do and see, and she was used to being surrounded by thousands of people, even though she'd been very much alone since Cassie moved to Bentham.

A scraping sound came from close behind her, followed by the unmistakable sound of fast-moving footsteps.

She turned, intending to move to the side, when a hand clamped around her ponytail, jerking her backward against a hard chest.

It took a moment for her brain to catch up with what was happening, and by the time it did, her assailant had taken his beefy hand from her hair and clamped it over her mouth.

Addy fought her rising panic. Like any savvy city girl, she'd taken self-defense classes, but it had been a while since she'd brushed up. She'd never thought she'd actually have to use any of those techniques.

She tried to pull away, but the man's arm was like a vise around her neck.

"Don't fight, and I won't hurt you," the man growled.

She didn't believe that for a minute. She'd left the small gun she carried for protection locked in her car's glove compartment, a decision she regretted now. Who'd have thought the streets of Bentham were more dangerous than Manhattan?

Well, she had no intention of going down without a fight, gun or no gun. She sent up a quick prayer and fisted her hands at the same time a yell came from somewhere in the night.

SHAWN WEST STOPPED at an intersection not far from the offices of the company he'd been sent to investigate.

Half a block away, on the opposite side of the street, a Black woman strolled toward him.

She was too far away to see her clearly, but the tailored slacks, black wool peacoat and dark gray loafers marked her as a professional, probably on her way home from work. A feeling of familiarity washed over him, but he quickly dismissed it. Despite its proximity to Manhattan, he'd never been to or met anyone from Bentham before.

A figure clad in black, a man based on the figure's height and size, peeled away from a darkened doorway as the woman approached the far street corner. The man grabbed the woman by the hair and wrapped his arm around her neck.

Shawn sprang from the Yukon.

He raced toward the man and woman, yelling as he did. "Hey!"

The man looked up, surprise on his face. The darkness, combined with the baseball cap the man wore, didn't allow Shawn a good look at the man's face. His arm stayed around the woman's neck, but his grip loosed enough that the woman's feet touched the ground again.

She took advantage of her assailant's distraction. Bracing herself, she bent her right leg and drove her heel back into the man's knee.

Her courage impressed him even as he put on a burst of speed, knowing that her fighting back had the potential to further aggravate her attacker. Shawn kept his eyes on the struggling pair.

The man's arms fell from around her, and he let out a torrent of curses Shawn could hear clearly from a block away.

"Help!" the woman's scream echoed off the empty buildings.

The man reached for the woman again.

"Hey!" Shawn yelled again. "Leave her alone!"

The man seemed to finally realize that Shawn wasn't just going to mind his own business and walk away.

He backed up, flinging the woman to the ground with another curse and fleeing.

Shawn slowed as he approached the woman. She lay on the pavement facing away from him on her side, coughing in an attempt to catch her breath. He scanned her body, looking for injuries. She didn't appear to be seriously hurt, but he still couldn't see her face.

Shawn glanced around the corner where the man had disappeared. The darkened doorways and parked vehicles along the street made for several good places to hide. He saw no one.

His heart pounding from exertion and adrenaline, Shawn turned back to the woman's side.

The feeling of familiarity struck him again, and when she pushed up to a sitting position, he understood why.

"Addy?"

Now she turned her gorgeous brown eyes on him, shock shining in them.

Her shoulders relaxed when he stepped out of the circle of light that engulfed her. "Shawn? What...what are you doing here?"

He and Addy Williams had spent an incredible weekend together six months earlier at Ryan's destination wedding. He'd tried to see her again after they'd returned to New York, but she hadn't answered any of his calls.

"Are you okay?" Shawn asked, ignoring her question for one he deemed more important at the moment.

He squatted next to her.

"Yes." Addy's voice cracked, and she stopped,

clearing her throat before speaking again. "He didn't hurt me."

Fury that she could have been hurt rose in him, but he tamped it down. She looked shaken but otherwise okay.

"We should call the cops." Shawn reached into the pocket of his leather jacket before remembering he'd left his phone in his car.

Addy pushed to her feet and pulled the sides of her coat closed around her. "No. No cops. I'm fine."

He stood, wondering whether she'd hit her head in the fall. They had to report the assault. "We should call. That guy could attack someone else."

She chewed her plump bottom lip, and a spark of attraction shot through him despite the frown that marked her pretty face.

Several seconds passed before she nodded in assent.

"I left my phone in the car," Shawn said, tilting his head toward the Yukon idling at the stop sign, the driver's door still wide-open.

He wanted to get her into the truck to wait, just in case her assailant came back.

"You can use mine," she said, unlocking the phone with her thumb before handing it to him.

They walked together toward his car. Shawn assessed the woman beside him as he dialed.

Why didn't Addy want to call the police?
Why was she in Bentham?
And why didn't she want to call the police?

Chapter Two

It took less than ten minutes for two deputies to arrive. After getting the description of her attacker, the first deputy left to patrol the area in an attempt to find the attacker. The second requested Addy and Shawn return with him to the sheriff's department to give formal statements. Addy elected to ride with the deputy, needing a moment to process the shock of finding herself staring into the mesmerizing eyes of Shawn West. For a second, she'd thought she must be hallucinating. It had been a few months since the incredible weekend they'd spent at her friend Nadia's wedding to Shawn's brother Ryan in St. Bart.

She'd met Shawn at the rehearsal dinner, and they'd clicked immediately. They'd chatted throughout dinner, then taken a moonlit stroll on the beach. Dancing at the reception under the stars, Shawn holding her close, she'd forgotten all about her vow to forgo romance in favor of her career. She'd invited Shawn back to her room, where they'd spent the entire night and most of the following day in bed.

And then she'd gone back to her real life in New York and completely ghosted him.

Addy wasn't sure whom she dreaded facing more: Sheriff Roger Donovan or Shawn West.

She pressed her palms against her forehead and groaned.

"Are you okay, ma'am?" The deputy glanced over at her.

"Yes. Sorry." Addy smiled weakly. "It's just been a day."

The deputy returned her smile with one of his own. He pulled the cruiser into a parking lot adjacent to a utilitarian brown building. Stone signage on the small grassy patch in front of the building proclaimed it the Bentham County Sheriff's Department.

SHAWN MET ADDY and the deputy at the front door. The three of them entered, and the deputy led them to a reception desk.

Addy stole a sly glance at Shawn as he signed in.

Six foot three and broad shouldered, he was a man who got noticed by men and women alike when he entered a room. Despite the cold temperatures, he wore a black leather jacket that looked as if it was molded to fit his powerful arms. Underneath the jacket, a gray shirt accentuated well-defined pecs and tailored slacks hugged a tight bottom. A thin dusting of stubble covered the rich brown skin along his jaw.

A fleeting memory of dotting kisses along that jaw brought a surge of heat to her cheeks. She quickly pushed the memory from her mind.

After they signed in, the deputy had them take a seat before he disappeared behind a thick gray door. A row of green folding chairs comprised the waiting area in the small lobby. The chairs faced a long metal desk topped with clear Plexiglas, no doubt bulletproof.

She took a seat next to Shawn, struggling to come up with something to say. He saved her by speaking first.

"You sure you're okay?" Shawn looked at her with concern in his eyes.

"Yes, thank you for helping me back there." Remembering that he'd never answered her question from earlier, she asked again. "What are you doing in Bentham?"

"You're welcome. I'm here on business," he responded without giving any further details.

The deputy's return stopped her from probing more.

"Ms. Williams. Mr. West. The sheriff is ready for you now."

Shawn stood and waited for Addy to move ahead of him. They followed the deputy down a long hallway, past a large room where other officers sat staring at computers or talking on the phone. She'd spoken with Sheriff Roger Donovan earlier that day and was surprised when the deputy stopped several doors short of the sheriff's office.

Addy felt her shoulders stiffen, but she followed the deputy into an interrogation room, Shawn at her heels. She'd never been in an interrogation room before, but it looked like the ones she'd seen on television. Soft padding, ripped in several places, covered the lower section of the wall. A rectangular table took up most of the small space, its faux-wood top chipped at one corner.

She settled herself next to Shawn again, tension coiled in her body.

If Shawn felt anxious at all, he didn't show it. He sat, legs spread, his hands on his thighs, a slight smile on his lips. Cool, calm and collected. And incredibly sexy.

The deputy excused himself, and less than a moment later a man in his late fifties with a full beard gone mostly gray entered the room.

Sheriff Donovan dropped a yellow legal pad and pen on the table. "Ms. Williams, I'm sorry to see you under those circumstances. I take it you weren't hurt?"

"Thank you, Sheriff. I'm fine," Addy answered stiffly.

"Good to hear." Sheriff Donovan nodded. "I have to say, I was surprised to learn you were still in town." The sheriff watched her with raised eyebrows.

She hadn't told the sheriff she planned to stay in town and look for Cassie on her own since he'd made it clear he would be of little help. She needed to find irrefutable evidence that Cassie hadn't just taken off, then she could force the sheriff to take action.

Sheriff Donovan's stare hadn't wavered. An intimidation tactic—one she was familiar with from negotiating her fair share of corporate mergers.

She held the sheriff's gaze, saying nothing.

Several seconds ticked by before the sheriff blinked and turned to Shawn. "And you must be the gentleman who saved Ms. Williams?"

Shawn's lips turned up into a cocky smile that matched his body language. "She saved herself. I just called your guys."

Sheriff Donovan scratched his jaw, his gaze shooting back to Addy, a look of disbelief on his face. "So how 'bout you folks tell me about the trouble you had tonight."

"I was walking back to my hotel after stopping for dinner when a man attacked me."

"And what hotel would that be?"

"The Madison Hotel downtown."

One of the sheriff's eyebrows rose. "That's a bit of a walk."

Addy shrugged. "I don't mind the cold, and I needed the time to clear my head."

Which wasn't totally untrue. She didn't mind the cold, but she'd been canvassing the area around Cassie's job and apartment, hoping someone had information that would help find her.

"Go on." Sheriff Donovan motioned with the pen in his hand.

"I'd just left the restaurant, headed back to my hotel. A man grabbed me from behind. He put his hand over my mouth and told me not to struggle."

The yellow legal pad sat in front of the sheriff untouched.

"Is that when Mr. West came along?"

She nodded. "Yes."

Sheriff Donovan turned to Shawn. "And I take it you intervened?"

"I was a half block away, about to turn onto the street when I saw Addy being attacked," Shawn answered.

Sheriff Donovan's brows drew together over

his nose. "Would have been wiser to dial 911." His gaze moved from Addy to Shawn and back. "You could have gotten both of you killed."

"I'm a PI. I know how to handle myself."

"A private eye?" Sheriff Donovan scowled.

Shawn nodded.

"Well, Mr. Private Eye, in my town the sheriff's office handles crime and private investigators chase cheating spouses."

Shawn glared.

The conversation was quickly devolving into a competition between the two men, but Addy had better things to do with her time.

"Getting back to tonight," Addy said pointedly, "Shawn yelled loud enough to catch the guy's attention and give me the opportunity to land a kick to his shin."

Addy recounted the rest of the details, thankful that the sheriff's focus no longer seemed to be on her acquaintance with Shawn. She wasn't comfortable explaining their relationship to a stranger. She wasn't even sure she could explain it to herself at this point.

"Did you get a look at him?" Sheriff Donovan asked, finally picking up his pen.

Addy shook her head. "No. He grabbed me from behind. I never saw his face."

"And what about you?" The sheriff turned to Shawn. "Did you get a look at this guy?"

"Only a glimpse. I doubt I could reliably identify him." Shawn's expression turned dark. "He took off when he saw me."

Sheriff Donovan turned his attention back to Addy. "Did he reach for your purse? Take anything of value before he ran off?"

"No." Addy tilted her head, thinking.

Why would a mugger attack her and not take her purse or wallet? He might have seen her leaving the restaurant and figured she had to have money or a credit card on her, but she'd been some blocks away from the restaurant when he attacked. A darker thought jumped into the forefront of her mind.

Addy knew the sheriff didn't think there was anything nefarious behind Cassie's disappearance, but Addy couldn't ignore the possibility that tonight's attack could be related.

Sheriff Donovan set his pen down. "I have to tell you, you haven't given me much to go on here."

The tone of the sheriff's voice piqued Addy's ire. "Does that mean you won't investigate?"

Sheriff Donovan's face turned hard. "The department will investigate as it does any complaint we receive."

"Sheriff, I don't think this guy was trying to rob me. I don't know why, but I think he was after me. Have you made any progress at all on locating my sister?"

"Ms. Williams, I assure you I am doing everything I can." Sheriff Donovan paused for a beat, looking at her over the tops of his rimless spectacles. "But your sister isn't a local."

Already frustrated by the sheriff's lack of urgency about Cassie's disappearance, she had to fight back the fury that rose inside at his comment. Beside her, Shawn tensed.

"I don't know why that should matter. Cassie has lived in Bentham for six months now. Does not having lived here longer make her disappearance less of a priority for you?"

Sheriff Donovan's gaze hardened. "I didn't say that," he ground out. "Small towns aren't for everyone. Someone like your sister, someone who's used to a big city like New York," he added quickly, "might find it hard to adapt. If your sister didn't go back to New York, maybe she tried another big city like Boston or Philly."

She knew what the sheriff was getting at. He'd talked to Cassie's roommate and boss.

Addy narrowed her gaze on the sheriff. "I don't believe my sister would just up and move without telling me."

"All her things were gone," the sheriff said, his arms spread wide as if the missing items proved his point.

Addy knew differently. Cassie hadn't mentioned a thing about moving back to New York or anywhere else for that matter in any of the phone calls or texts the sisters had shared over the last few weeks.

Addy shook her head, trying once again to get through the lawman's thick skull. "If Cassie moved back to New York, why hasn't she returned any of my calls? And where is she now? It's not as if she has anywhere to live in New York other than with me."

"Maybe she's staying with friends." She shook her head, and the sheriff sighed. "Tell me again why your sister moved to Bentham in the first place," he said, ignoring her question.

Once again she pushed back her frustration with the sheriff. Getting on his bad side wouldn't help her find Cassie, and that was all that was important to her at the moment. Gritting her teeth, she said, "Cassie wanted to take some time off before starting college in the fall. Experience the real world."

Sheriff Donovan nodded his head, taking notes, although she'd already told him all this when she'd called last week to make the missing person report and again when she'd spoken to him earlier that day.

"Bentham was close enough to New York that she could come home to visit whenever she wanted but far enough that she felt like she was out on her own."

"Didn't you tell me before that your father passed away recently?" The sheriff flipped through the pages in his notebook, presumably looking for the notes he'd taken during their last meeting.

"Yes, this past February, a few months before Cassie moved to town."

Their father had passed away seven months ago, but that didn't stop a fresh wave of grief from swelling in her chest. Shawn's hand moved to cover hers on the table, and the compassion she saw in his eyes nearly broke her.

Ryan and Nadia's wedding had taken place a month after her father's death and a year after her divorce. Addy didn't need to be a therapist to see the connection between these events and her one and only one-night stand. That was one of the reasons she hadn't returned his calls when she'd gotten back to New York. That and the butterflies that fluttered in her stomach whenever she thought about having him in her life beyond that single weekend.

She quickly directed her gaze back to the sheriff.

Sheriff Donovan set his pen on top of his pad and folded his hands in front of him.

"Sometimes people do weird things after a

loss." His gaze flicked to Shawn's hand, which still covered hers on the table. "Did your sister ever mention hurting herself?"

Addy pressed her lips together, afraid of what she might say if she spoke at the moment. She knew grief made people act out of character. But there was no way Cassie would ever do anything to hurt herself or anyone else.

"No." Addy shook her head vehemently.

Like Addy, Cassie grieved their father's death. She'd insisted on taking the internship with Spectrum to get real-world work experience before college. But Addy suspected that the move was as much about Cassie needing some space to process her grief and get away from all the memories of their father that still lingered in New York.

Addy didn't think of herself as a pessimist, but she was more of a realist than her father and sister. Although their father had tried to remain upbeat and hopeful while he fought the cancer, she'd been aware not too long after their father's diagnosis that the prognosis was bleak.

Cassie had a much tougher time dealing with the death of their father from cancer, months before her high school graduation. She'd held fast to hope that her father could beat the cancer right up until the end. A miracle that had never come.

With one month left in her senior year, Cassie had become depressed and nearly despondent. Her grades had taken a precipitous dive, although luckily, her GPA was strong enough to withstand the hit, and she'd already gotten her acceptance to MIT for the fall. When Cassie announced she'd deferred her college start date and wanted to move out of the city, Addy had thought it was a good idea, hopeful that the change would give her sister some much-needed time to grieve and heal before starting the next phase of her life.

Now she wondered if she'd live to regret supporting Cassie's decision to come to Bentham.

Sheriff Donovan used both hands to remove his glasses, laying them on his open notebook.

"Look, why don't you go on back to New York? Most likely your sister will turn up there a few days from now. I'll call you if I have anything to report."

The sheriff sent her a tight smile that Addy interpreted to mean he was done with both the Williams sisters and their problems.

Addy leaned forward, pressing her palms into the table and enunciating each word so the sheriff didn't miss a syllable.

"My sister did not just leave this town of her own volition. She's in trouble, and I'm not going anywhere until I've found her."

Chapter Three

It was nearly midnight by the time Shawn had settled into his room at the Madison Hotel. He would have to pay a fee since he'd canceled his original reservation at a nearby hotel so late, but instinct urged him to stick close to Addy. Something in his gut told him the attack on her tonight hadn't been a run-of-the-mill mugging.

Not that Addy's life was any of his business. She'd made that pretty clear by not returning any of the phone calls or texts he'd sent after their night together.

So why had he gotten a room at her hotel?

His phone rang before he could work out a satisfactory answer to that question. He didn't need to see the screen to know the call came from his older brother Ryan.

"'Ello," Shawn answered.

"Why haven't you been answering your phone? Are you there yet?" Ryan asked without preamble.

"I'm great, thanks. The drive was lovely," Shawn deadpanned, attempting to cut through some of the tension coming from Ryan's end of the call.

The loud, exaggerated sigh on the other end of the line was an increasingly familiar, and annoying, sound.

Ryan was indisputably the most serious of his brothers, which made him well suited to the position of president of West Investigations, but Ryan was also the most dramatic of the four West brothers.

Their father, James West Sr., had founded West Investigations, although he was semiretired and only saw a select few clients now. James Sr. liked to joke he'd reached the age where he could earn his money on the golf course, and Shawn and Ryan didn't disagree. They'd taken over the reins at West since their two older brothers' interests lay elsewhere.

Maybe it was the added pressure of being newly married with a baby on the way, but Ryan had been riding everyone at West harder than usual, Shawn in particular.

"Shawn, this is serious. Intellus Communications is one of our largest clients, and they will be in major legal and financial trouble if they don't find out who's counterfeiting their computer chips."

Shawn rolled his eyes even though his brother couldn't see it.

"Relax, Ry. I'm here and everything is under control."

He'd been scoping out the headquarters of Spectrum Industries, one of the businesses West had identified as possibly being involved in the corporate espionage against Intellus, when he'd seen Addy being attacked. Spectrum had two other business addresses, warehouses where they made their computer chips, that he still needed to check out.

"Good. Whoever's behind this has to have knowledge of and regular access to the manufacturing side of things as well as the management side. That suggests someone fairly high up in the company if Spectrum is behind this."

Shawn didn't bother responding. They'd gone over all this before he left for Bentham.

Zelig Ernst, CEO of Intellus and longtime client of West Security, had called Shawn from Intellus's headquarters in Silicon Valley this morning in a panic. Counterfeit computer chips with Intellus's logo had popped up all over the country. Ernst had ordered an investigation into their factory's production that had determined that the chips weren't coming from Intellus. Based upon the geographic location where most of the chips appeared to have entered the sales stream, Intellus had narrowed the possible source to two competitors in the market, one of which was Spectrum.

Intellus had hired West to investigate the two suspect companies and obtain proof of the guilty party. Ernst wanted to go to the police and the public with evidence that Intellus was a victim and had nothing to do with the fraud. So far Intellus's clients that had received fraudulent chips were willing to give the company the benefit of the doubt and a little bit of time to figure things out. Ernst wasn't sure that would hold if another batch of counterfeits made it into the market.

Shawn hesitated for a moment, considering whether to tell Ryan about the earlier incident with Addy. Before he could make up his mind, Ryan began speaking again.

"We don't have a lot of time. There's likely to be another batch of counterfeits in the market in a few days." The counterfeits appeared to flow into the market like clockwork every six weeks for the last three months, which only gave Intellus three days before the next batch of chips were scheduled to show up if the counterfeiters stayed on schedule.

Shawn bit back his irritation. He'd be the

first to admit that Ryan shouldered more of the administrative weight of running the company. But Shawn knew he was a damn good private investigator and had brought several new clients into the firm, including Intellus, in the four years since James Sr.'s retirement.

"I know that, Ry. I was on the call with Ernst just like you were. I'm on it. Gideon is checking out the other possible source, and I'm already in Bentham. If either of these companies is the source of the counterfeits, we'll nail them."

Ryan blew out a breath. "Good. When we find these guys, every company in the city will look to us for corporate cybersecurity."

Shawn worked his jaw, trying to lessen the tension there. "I know. I got this. You know I care about the company as much as you do."

"You need to be laser focused on this case."

"I got it, Ry," Shawn bit out. "It's late. I'm turning in for the night." He ended the call without saying goodbye.

They were long overdue for a discussion about Shawn's role within the company, but it would have to wait. He'd handle his job, hopefully finding out quickly if Spectrum was involved in the fraud.

And he'd keep an eye out for Addy while he was in Bentham, because something told him she was going to need it.

CRISP EARLY-MORNING AIR swept over Shawn's face as he walked back to the hotel from the café where he'd picked up breakfast. He strolled through the lobby without drawing so much as a glance from the desk clerk, having made a mental note of the room number Addy gave Donovan at the police station the evening before.

The sheriff had received an emergency call right after Addy had declared she wasn't leaving Bentham without Cassie, and Shawn had given her a lift back to the hotel. She'd remained stoic, her fury at Donovan still hot on the drive to the hotel. Not that he blamed her. Donovan certainly didn't appear to be taking Cassie Williams's disappearance too seriously. Still, Shawn had figured it wasn't the best time to explain his impromptu fib or to convince Addy to continue playing along with it.

After getting over the shock of seeing Addy again, he'd realized his plan for keeping a low profile while in Bentham was blown. He'd had no choice but to reveal his occupation when Donovan collected his personal information for the formal statement. Although he'd declined to give specifics regarding his stay in Bentham, New York City private investigators didn't just turn up in small-town Bentham for no reason. Shawn's concern now wasn't just with finding the source of Intellus's fraudulent chips, but also helping Addy find her missing sister and keep her out of danger. After all, he wasn't about to leave Addy to investigate on her own, even though she was clearly able to handle herself. He'd been surprised and impressed with how she'd taken on her attacker. There was nothing sexier than a beautiful woman who could take care of herself.

Shawn gave himself a mental slap. He wasn't going to go there. Addy clearly wasn't interested in him, and he wasn't about to put himself out there a second time and have her dance all over his heart. She needed help finding her sister, and quite possibly protection. Those were jobs he knew how to do, so he'd offer his help, but that was all.

He balanced the coffee holder and a bag of food in one hand and rapped on Addy's door with his free hand. A full minute passed without any sound from within the room. He knocked again, harder this time, worry furrowing his brow. It was early, not quite eight, but he'd wanted to make sure he caught her. Maybe she'd gone down to the hotel restaurant for breakfast.

After a moment more, he turned away from the room, heading for the restaurant, when the locks clicked open. The door swung inward, and Addy peered around the side of the door at him.

"What are you doing here?" Addy asked in a voice still heavy with sleep.

His blood heated at her sultry rasp.

Ignoring the spark of attraction, he flashed a smile. "Just being a good neighbor. My room is down the hall. I bought breakfast," he said, holding up the coffees and the bag.

"What time is it?" She swung the door open, and he just about stopped breathing.

Her New York Knicks T-shirt stopped at midthigh, revealing what seemed like miles of smooth brown skin ending in fiery-red toenails. She crossed her arms, pulling her shirt tight across her chest and revealing curves that had his mouth feeling like it had been stuffed with cotton.

He swallowed hard and cleared his throat. "Ah, it's almost eight."

Addy's eyes widened. "I never sleep this late."

"Can I come in?"

Her eyes narrowed, and he shifted so he wouldn't get hit if she slammed the door in his face.

He thrust one of the coffees at her, hoping the offering would tip her calculus in his favor. He was rewarded.

She grabbed the coffee, closing her eyes and inhaling deeply before taking a long sip.

"Okay." Addy's dark brown eyes fluttered open, sending an electric charge through him. "You can come in."

She turned away from the door and strode to the round table pushed into a corner of the room.

He blew out a ragged breath and followed.

Unlike the suite he'd reserved three floors above, Addy's room needed renovations, but it was clean and had all the expected amenities—two queen beds; a square side table between them; a flat-screen television atop a wide, six-drawer dresser; Wi-Fi and USB hookups. One of the two beds had a laptop at its center with a handful of papers scattered around it. Rumpled bedsheets covered the other mattress.

Addy set her coffee on the table. "I need a minute," she said, grabbing her travel bag and carrying it to the bathroom.

He caught a glimpse of a large rectangular mirror over a white countertop before the bathroom door closed.

Shawn sat at the table and reached in the bag for one of the two breakfast sandwiches he'd picked up on the way to the hotel. The small stack of papers perched on the edge of the table fluttered to the floor.

He picked them up, glancing at the sheet on top. A copy of the missing person report for Cassie Williams, dated five days earlier.

Shawn's eye traveled down the page, drawn to the name of Cassie's employer.

Spectrum Industries.

From the bathroom, he heard the sound of the toilet flushing and the sink faucet turning on. Addy would be back any second.

He righted the stack of papers, searching his memory for whether Addy had mentioned her sister worked at Spectrum during their chat with the sheriff last evening. He recalled her saying Cassie had moved to Bentham for an internship, but not where. Cassie's disappearance could be unconnected to his case, but he didn't believe in coincidence.

The bathroom door opened, leaving him no more time to ponder the information he'd just learned.

Addy walked back across the room to the table, and Shawn couldn't help being disappointed that she'd pulled a pair of yoga pants over her shapely legs.

"Thanks for the coffee," she said, sitting in the chair across from him and pulling her legs up under her.

"I bought breakfast, too." He pushed the second sandwich across the table.

She unwrapped it and frowned. "What is this?"

"Egg whites and spinach on a whole-grain English muffin."

She shot a steely look across the table and slid the sandwich back toward him. "You can go now."

Shawn rolled his eyes. "Just try it," he said, pushing the sandwich at her again.

Addy's cell phone rang, and she went to the bedside table where it lay charging. She frowned, pressing her finger to the phone's screen and carrying it back to the table. It buzzed in her hand as she reclaimed her seat. She glanced at the phone again, her frown deepening.

"Everything okay?"

She smiled tightly. "Fine. You never answered my question. What are you really doing here?" She ignored the sandwich and reached for her coffee cup.

He wasn't ready to answer that question just yet, so he replied with his own. "How long has your sister been missing?"

She took another sip of coffee before responding. "I haven't heard from Cassie in more than a week. The sheriff seemed content to believe she's just picked up and moved, but I know Cassie wouldn't do that without telling me."

"How old is Cassie?" Shawn asked, unwrapping his sandwich.

"Nineteen. She's taking a gap year before starting MIT in the fall."

"And she chose to spend it in Bentham?" He failed to keep the skepticism from his voice.

Addy chuckled. "It's not exactly Paris, but I think she just needed a little space."

"You mentioned your father died recently."

She swallowed hard. "Yes. Cassie insisted her move from New York was about experiencing the real world before college, but I think she needed some space from all the memories of our father in the city."

"Could she have decided Bentham wasn't far enough away?"

Her hands curled into fists on top of the table. "If she was going to go somewhere, she would have told me or one of her friends. I reached out to all of them, and none have heard from her. Cassie would call to ask if I thought she should have vanilla bean ice cream or rocky road for dessert. Then eat both." She chuckled, and the smile that lit her dark brown eyes sent his heart stuttering. "She ran everything by me or one of her other friends. No way she'd move without mentioning it to anyone." She hit the table with her fist, punctuating the statement.

He had no doubt she believed what she said,

but everyone kept secrets, even from those they were closest to. Addy could be right about her sister, or she could be too close to the situation to see it clearly. The fact that Cassie worked for Spectrum and someone there might be engaged in major fraudulent activity added a layer of intrigue to the situation.

A pang of guilt shot through him, but he swept it away. West had promised Intellus they'd keep the fraud on a need-to-know basis for the time being, so telling Addy the truth about why he was in Bentham was out of the question. He couldn't be sure she'd let him stick close if she knew he thought Cassie could be involved in fraud. And he had every intention of sticking to her like glue, because if Cassie was involved, Addy could be in danger.

"So what do you think happened? Where do you think Cassie is?" Shawn asked.

Anguish flooded her face, and he had the sudden urge to wrap her in his arms. "I don't know." Her voice faltered, and she took a moment to steady herself before going on. "But Sheriff Donovan doesn't seem to care to find out, so I'm going to have to do it myself."

Definitely a strong woman.

"When you last heard from Cassie, did she sound worried or upset?"

"No." Addy picked at the English muffin,

popping a small piece into her mouth. "Why are you so interested?"

"Questions are an occupational hazard in my line of work."

"Yes, but you aren't my PI. I haven't hired you."

He raised an eyebrow. "I've been known to do some pro bono work."

Addy tilted her head, her eyes narrowed. "You're good at avoiding my questions. Eat your breakfast." She eyed her own English muffin before taking a bite. "How can you eat this? It tastes like sand mixed with seaweed."

He swallowed. "It's healthy. Did Cassie have a boyfriend?"

"You get to ask questions, but I don't?"

"You can ask. I just may not answer." He smiled to soften his words.

She took another small bite of her sandwich, then tossed the rest in the trash. "Why should I answer your questions if you don't answer mine?"

"Because I have experience finding missing people. I can help you if you let me." He tapped her to-do list for emphasis.

She studied him like the sharp negotiator he knew she was. He'd googled her after Ryan's wedding and learned she was an up-and-coming legal superstar. She'd been at the helm of a number of big mergers and acquisitions. According to the intel he'd been able to glean from his brother Brandon, Addy was on the fast track to partnership at her firm.

Seemingly having made up her mind to let him help, Addy finally answered. "Cassie was dating a guy named Ben. They worked together at Spectrum here in Bentham."

"What did she do at Spectrum?"

"I'm not sure, exactly. I know she thought the internship would help her careerwise. Cassie plans to get her degree in computer science."

His Spidey senses were tingling. There were way too many events converging around Spectrum—Addy's sister's disappearance and evidence that Spectrum was behind the fraudulent chips—to be mere coincidences.

He could use Cassie's disappearance as his in at Spectrum. Cassie's coworkers were more likely to talk to him if they thought he was helping her to find Cassie. It was a decent plan, though not perfect.

He slid a look across the table. Addy had twisted her shoulder-length brown hair into a bun and applied some shimmery powder to her cheeks. She looked fresh-faced and gorgeous.

"I have a proposal for you. I am in town doing a job for a client, but the client has demanded I keep the reason for my presence confidential."

Her eyes lit with understanding. "And you think I can help you do that."

Shawn grinned.

"I had planned to keep a low profile while in town, but that's out the window now. I need a reason to be in town."

"And you want me to be that reason? Even though you won't tell me what you are working on?" The corners of her mouth turned down.

"I can't tell you. But I can help you look into your sister's disappearance."

She chewed her bottom lip, studying the tabletop. "I don't know."

Shawn leaned back in the chair. In his experience, the best way to convince someone to do what he wanted them to do was to provide a sober recitation of the advantages. In this case, his main advantage was that Addy didn't have the skill or expertise to conduct a missing-person investigation. "I've handled several missing-person cases, and West Security is one of the best investigative firms in New York. You'll have all our resources at your disposal. Free of charge."

He waited while she thought it over, confident she'd accept the offer. Addy was a smart cookie, and more importantly, she was motivated to find her sister.

"Okay," she answered after a moment of hesitation. "But you have to get out now. I need to shower."

She stood, and he did the same.

He accepted the win and contemplated how he'd convince Ryan to devote West resources to their new pro bono case. It shouldn't be too hard. Ryan still owed him one from a year earlier when West had become involved in helping Nadia's brother get out from under the mob. It was time he collected on that IOU.

"Great. Thank you for doing this." He headed for the door. "If you pack your stuff, I'll move it to my room when you're ready and you can check out of this room."

Addy's eyes went wide. "Hang on. I didn't agree to share a room with you."

"Relax," he said, retreating to the door. "I have a suite." A one-room suite, but he'd sleep on the pullout couch in the living room. Addy's expression remained skeptical. "You'll have your own room, but Cassie is missing and you've already been attacked once. I think it's safer for you if we stay in the same room."

Her nose wrinkled as if she'd smelled something foul, but she nodded finally. "I'll be ready when you get back."

He called Ryan as soon as he got back to the suite.

"You got anything yet?" Ryan answered without preamble.

"There may be something bigger than fraudulent computer chips going on here."

Shawn explained the situation with Addy, the attack on her last night and Cassie working for Spectrum and going missing.

"And you think all that is connected to our investigation."

"It would be one hell of a coincidence if it wasn't," Shawn answered, tossing his meager belongings back into his duffel bag and moving them out of the bedroom. The suite had a tiny powder room near the door that he could use for everything except showers.

Ryan swore under his breath. "You got a plan?"

Shawn explained his cover as a PI working with Addy to help her look for her sister.

"I don't mind using West resources to help her out, but don't forget why you're there. Intellus's job has to come first," Ryan clipped out.

"I got it." Shawn's voice came out sharper than he'd intended. Ryan treating him as if he didn't know how to do his job grated. As soon as this case was over, they were going to talk.

He gave Ryan Addy's and Cassie's full names

and asked for background checks on both before hanging up.

The look of anguish on Addy's face when he'd asked what she thought happened to Cassie flittered through his memory. He hadn't mentioned the likelihood of finding Cassie alive diminished exponentially every day, but he wasn't surprised that she seemed to be aware of that fact. Cassie had already been missing for nine days; that didn't bode well for finding her alive. But finding Cassie, dead or alive, would give Addy some closure; he could already tell she wasn't the type who'd be able to move on with her own life without knowing what had happened to her sister. Intellus's job would come first, but he'd also do everything in his power to find Cassie Williams.

Chapter Four

After Shawn left, Addy took a shower and packed before dialing a number that was becoming increasingly familiar to her. As with the last two times she'd called, Suri Bedingfield's phone rang until the voice mail kicked in. Biting back frustration, Addy left a third message for Cassie's roommate, then called up to Shawn's suite and checked out of her room.

She wasn't sure whether sharing a suite with Shawn was wise given their history and the attraction she still felt for him. In the end, the balance in her bank account and the bills waiting for her back home tipped the scales. That and the fact that she felt safe with him. The more she thought about the mugging, the more convinced she became that she hadn't been just a convenient victim. The attacker had targeted her specifically.

After helping her move her things to his suite, Shawn agreed that they should go see

Cassie's boss. On the short drive from the hotel to Spectrum, Addy relayed what little she knew about Caroline Webb, Cassie's boss, and Ben Konstam, Cassie's coworker and boyfriend. She'd purposely chosen a hotel not far from the center of downtown Bentham so she'd be close to Cassie's office and the duplex where she rented an apartment.

Located in a midcentury limestone building, Spectrum's headquarters spanned a half block. Shawn parked in a nearby surface parking lot, and they took the elevator to Spectrum's seventh-floor offices. Since most of what she knew about tech companies came from the movies and television, she'd expected Spectrum's offices to be a bright space with lots of chrome and glass and hipster employees sipping lattes in their open-floor-plan offices.

The elevator doors opened into a typically dull office space with harsh overhead lighting and industrial-gray carpeting leading through a maze of corridors.

A middle-aged, red-haired woman in a tan sweater and cardigan sat behind the reception desk. "Welcome to Spectrum. How may I help you today?" she said with a practiced smile.

The receptionist gave Shawn the once-over, a reaction Addy found irritating even though the woman was at least two decades older than Shawn and her.

Shawn offered a smile but didn't speak. They'd discussed how they planned to approach Ms. Webb on the drive over. Since Addy had spoken with Caroline Webb over the phone the previous week, they'd decided she would take the lead. It would also be harder for Cassie's boss to refuse to speak to the sister of a missing employee.

"My name is Addy Williams. My sister, Cassie Williams, is an intern here. I'd like to speak to her boss, Caroline Webb, please?"

The woman tapped the keyboard a few times in front of her before her gaze shifted back to Addy. "Do you have an appointment?"

Addy smiled tightly. "I don't, but I'm hoping Ms. Webb has a bit of time to see me. You may be aware that my sister is missing, and I'm sure everyone here at Spectrum wants to do what they can to help locate her."

She had no compunction about using a little manipulation to get around Spectrum's gatekeeper.

"One moment, please."

The receptionist dialed a number, and after several seconds announced that "an Addy Williams and a gentleman" were there to see the person at the other end of the line. Moments later the receptionist replaced the phone's receiver and directed them to take the second right at the end of the hallway.

Addy and Shawn passed several smartly dressed employees in designer dresses and tailored suits, reminding Addy of the corridors of Covington and Baker and the stable of suits in her closet back in New York. Like at Covington and Baker, Spectrum's corridors were a labyrinth of passageways seemingly designed to be as confusing as possible.

Cassie's direct boss was the human resources director, Caroline Webb. She and Shawn finally found her office nestled in a far corner of the floor, between the men's room and what appeared to be the company break room.

A balding Caucasian man in an impeccably tailored blue suit and a white woman in a boxy gray dress greeted them.

The man, in his early seventies and round everywhere, held his hand out to Addy. "Ms. Williams, I'm Martin Raupp, CEO of Spectrum Industries."

Addy shook his hand.

Martin Raupp held himself with the self-assurance of a man with power. "Caroline called to tell me you were here. Everyone at Spectrum is just distressed to hear that Cassie is missing, and we'll do whatever we can to help the police locate her safe and sound."

Martin Raupp's voice rang with sincerity. Addy was touched that he'd made a point to see her when he'd heard she was in the building.

"Thank you, Mr. Raupp. This is my friend Shawn West. He's a private investigator, and he's helping me to find Cassie."

Caroline Webb pressed her lips together. Heat rose in Addy's cheeks, but she didn't take her hand from Shawn's.

Mr. Raupp clapped his hands together in front of him. "Well, I'll leave you in Ms. Webb's capable hands. Please know that my wife, Madeline, and I are praying for Cassie's safe return."

He flashed one more smile their way and exited the office.

Caroline motioned them to sit. Addy lowered herself into the chair next to Shawn and opposite her desk. A full-figured woman in her mid to late fifties, Caroline had pulled her gray-brown hair up into a tight bun at the crown of her head.

"Ms. Webb, thank you for seeing me without an appointment. I'm sorry to barge in on you like this," Addy offered, not feeling a bit sorry but hoping to smooth any ruffled feathers.

Caroline pursed her lips again, although

Addy couldn't tell if it was in annoyance or merely a habit. "Not a problem. I'm sorry to hear that Cassie is missing. I shall do anything I can to help."

Caroline Webb had a pronounced British accent. She shot a glance at Shawn, although Addy noted it wasn't more benign than the receptionist's assessment had been.

"I'm hoping you can help me fill in some of Cassie's movements in the days before she went missing. Sheriff Donovan said that Cassie had resigned her internship, but Cassie never spoke of it to me."

Caroline nodded. "Yes, I was quite surprised, to be honest with you. Cassie seemed happy, and she was well-liked."

"What exactly did she do as an intern?" Shawn asked, rubbing his thumb against the back of Addy's hand and sending little shivers down her spine. She stole a glance at him, wondering if he knew what his touch did to her. His gaze stayed focused on Caroline Webb.

Get a grip. You need to focus here.

"Cassie did whatever we needed her to do. Mostly filing and other paperwork. But because she was so interested in computer science, I made it a point that she should be allowed to shadow the engineers over at the factory twice a week." Caroline folded her hands atop her desk primly.

Shawn's grip on Addy's hand tightened ever so slightly. She looked over at him again and saw that his body had also tensed, although for the life of her she couldn't figure out why. It made perfect sense that Cassie would jump at the chance to hang out with computer engineers, since that was what she'd be studying once she got to MIT.

"Has she had any trouble at work lately?" Shawn asked, their agreement that Addy would take the lead apparently forgotten.

Ms. Webb shook her head. "No. As I said, Cassie was very well-liked around here. A hard worker. Always to work on time and willing to stay late to meet deadlines if necessary."

That sounded just like Cassie and proved she hadn't simply quit without notice, as far as Addy was concerned.

"My sister was dating a Spectrum employee who worked in Spectrum's factory. Ben Konstam," Addy said, making sure not to let how she felt about Cassie's choice in boyfriend show on her face.

Addy had had reservations about her sister dating a coworker. She'd warned Cassie against starting a workplace romance, but Cassie was Cassie. Stubborn. Bullheaded. Determined to live life on her terms and make her own mistakes. Cassie had accused Addy of not wanting her to date Ben because he wasn't white-collar enough. Addy had denied it, hurt that Cassie would suggest such a thing, although when she dug down deep inside, she couldn't deny that the education and potential income disparity likely had something to do with it. Addy's divorce had devastated her, especially when she'd realized the only reason her ex-husband, Phillip, had married her was for her law firm salary. She didn't want Cassie to end up in the same situation.

Caroline's mouth turned down in a frown. "I am aware." She didn't speak for a moment, then added, "Mr. Konstam no longer works in the factory. He's been promoted to management."

"He works in this building?" Addy asked, surprised. Cassie hadn't mentioned Ben getting a promotion.

She glanced at Shawn but found his expression unreadable.

"Down the corridor." Caroline Webb inclined her head toward the hall beyond her office. "You passed his office on the way here."

That was perfect. They could kill two birds with one visit.

"What did Cassie say when she quit?" Addy asked, directing the conversation back to the days right before Cassie disappeared. "I mean, did she give you a reason why she was leaving the internship almost eight months early?"

"Well, I didn't speak to Cassie. I found her letter of resignation, effective immediately, on my desk one morning." Caroline scowled, no doubt aggrieved at the unprofessional way Cassie had supposedly resigned.

To Addy, it was only further evidence that something was very wrong. Their father had instilled a strong work ethic in both of his daughters. There's no way Cassie would quit a job without notice and without talking to her boss in person.

Addy's heartbeat ticked up with an increase in the fear she felt for her sister. "Did you try calling her?"

Caroline's back stiffened. "I did," Ms. Webb answered, a haughty undertone creeping into her voice.

Shawn squeezed Addy's hand. "I don't think Addy was implying you did anything wrong." Shawn flashed a boyish smile. "We're just trying to get a clear picture of things. Were you ever able to speak with Cassie?"

Caroline's shoulders relaxed, but she didn't return Shawn's smile. "Miss Williams never returned my calls. It wasn't like her as far as I knew her, but young people these days are so self-involved." She shook her head, unhappiness with the youth of the day chiseled in her expression. "I simply filed the paperwork to terminate her employment. Now, I truly am sorry, but I must get on with my workday."

"One more question. Could I have a look at Cassie's resignation letter?" Addy said.

Caroline shook her head. "I'm sorry. That wouldn't be appropriate, as it's part of an employee's personnel file."

Addy scooted forward in her chair.

"You wouldn't have any way of knowing if Cassie's signature was genuine. I'd know if it was a forgery."

Caroline's head continued its side-to-side motion.

"The sheriff could get a warrant," Shawn said, as if the idea had just occurred to him. "There is an active missing-person case open. But that would mean formally engaging the company in a legal process, and you know how cops can be. If they start asking for one thing, they'll ask for a dozen extra things."

Caroline bit her bottom lip, her expression thoughtful.

The woman seemed to be fond of Cassie, but Addy could tell she was at war with herself over breaking the rules. A rule follower herself, Addy understood the struggle, but if breaking the rules helped locate Cassie, she would break them all and induce whoever she needed to do the same.

"Please?" Addy pleaded. "Just a glance at the signature, that's all. You said yourself that re-signing this way wasn't something you'd have expected from Cassie. What if she didn't really sign that letter?" Addy pleaded.

Caroline nodded and turned to the computer at the edge of her desk and hit several keys. The printer behind her whirred to life.

She reached behind her and snatched the paper the printer spit out.

"We don't keep much paper around these days." Aside from a small stack of files on her desk, there was no paper in the office, not even file cabinets that might have held paper files. "Everything is scanned to the system, then sent off-site."

Caroline handed the paper from the printer across the desk to Addy.

A copy of Cassie's resignation letter.

Addy skipped over the text of the letter, going straight to the signature. She evaluated every loop, line and dotted *i* for any sign that the name at the bottom of the letter hadn't been penned by her sister.

After a minute of inspection, her heart sank. She recognized the signature as Cassie's.

Chapter Five

Shawn could tell by the look on Addy's face when she read the letter that it was Cassie's signature. Caroline didn't have any more information to give them, so they said their goodbyes.

They retraced their steps back toward the exit, agreeing without words to drop in on Ben while they were in the building. Shawn scanned the office doors on the left side of the hallway while Addy did the same for the doors on the right. As he did, he thought about what Caroline had said about Cassie and her role at Spectrum. He hadn't been able to control the involuntary twitch of his hand when he'd heard Cassie worked on both the management and production sides of the company. And he knew Addy had noticed.

Cassie fit the profile for a Spectrum employee involved in the fraud. Based on what he knew about her, Cassie seemed to have the knowledge of computer hardware and the process of chip making necessary as well as the access to carry out the fraud. Not that he thought for a minute she could carry out a fraud like this on her own. But with a boyfriend that had contacts within Spectrum spanning years? It would also explain why a nineteen-year-old from New York, on her way to one of the premier universities in the country, would put it all on hold to take an internship in a small town.

He and Addy finally found the door with Ben's name on it. Shawn knocked on the open door, drawing the attention of the broad-shouldered white man sitting behind the desk. He looked younger than Shawn had expected, although he knew from what Addy had told him on the way over that Ben was twenty-six. He could tell the age difference between Cassie and Ben bothered her.

Ben's light brown hair curled around the back of his neck to skim the top of his ill-fitting suit. He looked like a teenage kid who'd borrowed his dad's suit for a job interview.

Addy stepped around Shawn into the office. "Ben Konstam? My name is Addy Williams. I'm Cassie's sister. Do you have a moment?"

"Of course," Ben said, rising but remaining behind his desk. "Have you heard anything from Cassie?"

Ben's words had been right, but there'd been

no emotion behind them. A glance at the frown marring Addy's pretty face had Shawn thinking she felt the same way.

"No. That's why we're here," Addy answered. She quickly introduced Shawn before turning to the reason they were there. "I'm hoping you can shed some light on the situation."

Ben spread his hands in front of him. "Anything I can do, I will. I care for Cassie very much." He motioned for them to have a seat in the square-backed chairs positioned across from his desk.

Shawn sank into the chair, watching Ben closely.

"How did you and Cassie meet?" Shawn started the questioning off, taking Ben's measure. He wanted to see if Ben's description of his relationship with Cassie matched up with what Addy had said.

"I was working on the loading docks when Cassie first started with Spectrum. There was a mix-up in some paperwork for one of the shipments. Cassie brought the correct invoices over." Ben's voice remained emotionless.

For a man with a missing girlfriend, he was uncharacteristically nonplussed.

"This building has loading docks?" Shawn pressed.

Ben gave a half smile. "Not here. This is the

corporate office of Spectrum. There's another building where the sausage is made, so to speak." Ben chuckled at his joke.

"And where is that building?"

Ben tilted his head to the side, his forehead scrunching. "Oh, not far, just about three miles outside town. It's impossible to get a large enough space for a reasonable rent downtown."

"Of course. It's too bad. I tinker with computers myself, and I'd hoped to get a chance to see how the sausage is made," Shawn said, hoping to allay any wariness.

A smug smile swelled across Ben's face and his chest puffed out. "Anytime you want to take a tour of the facility, just give me a call, and I'll set it up. I have an in with the guys in the warehouse since I used to be one of them. Just because I'm in the corporate suite doesn't mean I'll be forgetting my roots."

Shawn slid a glance at Addy, catching the suspicion in her eyes. Ben had just confirmed the lease that West's property search had turned up was in fact held on the factory, which was helpful to his case but did little to find Cassie.

"So you worked on the loading docks nine months ago. What did you do?" Shawn said, getting them back on track.

"I loaded the trucks and then delivered the chips to customers up and down the East Coast."

Ben picked up a pen and began tapping it against the top of the desk.

"From delivery driver to assistant shipping manager. That's a hell of a success story," Addy said.

"I got an associate's degree in business management," Ben said defensively, jerking his head toward the framed diploma in the wall. "Spectrum is all about moving employees that prove themselves up through the ranks. Employee retention and all that."

"When was the last time you saw Cassie?" Addy questioned.

"It's been a few weeks now." Ben tilted his head back, looking up at the ceiling as if searching for the date up there. Or avoiding making eye contact. "Yeah, more like a month ago."

Shawn's eyebrow rose. "Was it normal for you two to go that long without seeing each other?"

Ben's eyes darted around the room. "Normal? I mean, we weren't married, man. I don't know what she told you," Ben said, looking at Addy, "but things with us were casual-like."

Addy opened her mouth to speak, but Shawn sensed that whatever she was going to say wouldn't further the conversation.

"Did Cassie seem worried?" Shawn spoke up

before Addy. "Maybe preoccupied when you saw her last?"

Ben closed one eye, squinting in thought. "No, not that I remember."

"Suri, Cassie's roommate, said Cassie told her she was moving back home to New York. Did Cassie mention a move to you?" Shawn pressed on.

"Yeah. I told the sheriff all this." Ben tapped the pen faster. "Cassie was ready to go home."

"Why didn't she tell me if she was coming back to New York?" Addy spat.

Ben shrugged. "Maybe she wanted to surprise you. Maybe she...she wanted to be in New York but didn't want to deal with family yet. I don't know, but I know she said she was going home."

Silence ensued as Ben looked down at his desk, avoiding Addy's disbelieving glare.

He was hiding something.

"What did Cassie do for Spectrum?" Shawn asked, hoping a different approach would yield more answers.

Ben tore his attention from the desktop.

"Filing. Answering the phone. Taking notes in meetings. She pretty much did whatever needed to be done." His answer matched what Caroline had said.

"Did she have problems with anyone at work

bothering her? Argue with anyone?" Shawn asked.

"No. Let's be honest, Cassie wasn't in a position to argue with anyone around here," Ben snapped. "It's not like she gave orders or was a supervisor. Look, I need to get back to work." Ben stood, indicating the end of the conversation.

Addy and Shawn followed suit, leaving Ben's office and heading down the corridor toward the elevators.

"He's not telling the truth," Addy said as soon as they were out of hearing distance of Ben's office. "Cassie would not have moved without talking to me."

"He definitely wasn't telling us everything, but that doesn't mean he had anything to do with Cassie's disappearance."

Addy shot him a murderous look. He was sure she was prepared to argue the point, but a petite woman stepped out of an office to their right before she could get started.

"Excuse me. You're Cassie's sister, right?" the woman asked.

"Yes. Addy Williams. This is Shawn West."

"I'm Claudia." The woman's gaze darted down the hall. She took a step back into her office, though not far enough to allow Shawn and Addy to enter.

"I debated saying anything, but if it was my sister—" Claudia wrung her hands.

Addy took a step forward. "Please, if you know anything that could help me find Cassie—"

"I overheard a conversation between Cassie and Ben. An argument, really. The day before Cassie went missing."

Shawn assessed the woman in front of him. She twisted her hands nervously in front of her.

"What were they arguing about?" Addy asked.

"Well, I don't want to get anyone in trouble." Claudia reached for her office door.

Addy slid forward, placing herself so the door could not be closed. "Please. It might help us find Cassie."

Claudia sighed. "I didn't hear much. Ben asked if they could talk about 'it,' and Cassie said no, they'd already talked and she had nothing more to say to him about it or them. She said they were through and she was going to do the right thing."

Claudia shook her head and wrung her hands more.

"And neither one of them mentioned what the 'it' they were talking about was?"

"Sorry, no. I didn't hear anything else. Cassie walked away from Ben then."

"Did Ben follow her?" Shawn asked.

The skin on Claudia's forehead creased. "I don't know. Neither of them walked directly past me, but I could hear Cassie's heels. That's how I knew she walked away. It's possible Ben followed her or he could have gone down the other hall there." She pointed to where the hall jutted off to the left.

"Did you tell Sheriff Donovan about the argument?"

"Oh, well, no. Like I said, I don't want to get anybody in trouble." Claudia edged back into her office.

Shawn had met too many people who didn't want to "get involved." If Claudia had told Donovan what she'd seen and heard, he might have taken Cassie's disappearance more seriously from the beginning. Shawn bit back his annoyance with the skittish woman.

"Telling the sheriff what you heard would be helpful."

"I'll think about it." This time Claudia did push the door until Addy had no choice but to move or be hit by it. The door clicked closed in their faces.

Shawn wouldn't be placing any bets on Claudia going to Donovan, but he made a mental note to pass on the information himself. Hopefully, Donovan would follow up.

"You think that's what Ben was holding

back? That he and Cassie argued right before she disappeared?" Addy said.

"It's possible. It might explain his obvious nervousness and reluctance to talk to us. As the boyfriend, he's already under the microscope. If it's known that he and Cassie weren't getting along, that makes him even more of a suspect."

"Let's go back and see what he has to say about it."

Ben's office was empty and dark when they returned.

"We need to go see Sheriff Donovan. Ben knows more than he's saying about Cassie's disappearance." Addy marched down the corridor and out of Spectrum's offices.

"Slow down," he said, following her. "We've got no evidence that Ben had anything to do with Cassie's disappearance."

She punched the elevator down button before whirling on him. "What are you talking about? He wouldn't have run out of here right after we talked to him if he had nothing to hide."

"We don't know why he left. He could have a lunch meeting." He raised his hands to stop the onslaught he felt coming. "I'm not saying I believe that, but we can come back later and question Ben again. Hopefully, we'll have more information then and we'll be able to confront him with some facts."

The elevator doors opened.

"Okay, how are we going to get this information?"

Shawn frowned, afraid she wasn't going to like his answer. "I don't know."

Chapter Six

Addy stayed silent until they'd stepped onto the sidewalk in front of the building. "Ben is lying."

Her skin felt as if thousands of needles were pricking it. What little control she had over her emotions was rapidly fraying. She didn't know why everyone was so quick to believe that Cassie had moved back to New York, but she knew that hadn't been her sister's plan. "Maybe Cassie broke up with him and he kidnapped her. It happens. We need to get Sheriff Donovan to search Ben's house."

Shawn's hand landed on her shoulder, holding her in place. "Hold on a minute."

"We don't have a minute." Addy shook his hand off her shoulder. "I know Cassie is still alive. I can sense it, but it feels like I'm running out of time to find her."

"Chasing after Ben isn't going to make him

tell you what he knows about Cassie's disappearance. If he knows anything."

"What do you mean, if he knows anything? Did you see how nervous and jittery Ben was?"

"I saw, but he could have been nervous about anything. Or a general nervousness could be his usual state of being."

She gaped at Shawn for a moment before turning and stalking away down the sidewalk. He was no better than the sheriff.

Tears pricked at the backs of her eyes, blurring her vision. "Agreeing to let you help me was a mistake."

She missed the dip in the sidewalk and stumbled. Strong arms latched on to her waist from behind, righting her before she fell.

"Are you okay?"

Addy twisted, looking up into Shawn's dark eyes. Desire sizzled between them. "Yes, I'm fine. I'm just hungry. I didn't have much breakfast." She shot him a look.

Shawn smiled wryly. "Look, let me buy you something to eat, and we can talk about our next steps."

She was anxious to find Ben and question him further. But a wave of light-headedness swept over her at the mention of food, making her glad his hands were still clasped around her waist. A couple of bites of whatever Shawn had brought to her hotel room this morning had not cut it.

"Okay, but I pick where we eat," she said, stepping out of his arms. As she did, a wave of regret swept through her.

Shawn West had the potential to uproot all her carefully laid plans. But would that be so bad?

Addy pushed the question from her mind and focused on her growling stomach.

She'd noticed a diner adjacent to the lot where they'd parked. She led Shawn back toward the parking lot now, stopping just before they reached it at double glass front doors with The Golden Spoon etched on them in gold.

Addy cocked an eyebrow, waiting to see if he'd complain.

He looked at the door warily but kept silent.

Addy reached for the door at the same time he did. Their hands touched, and another sizzle of electricity shot through her.

The sound of a clearing throat broke their reverie. Addy stepped into the diner, aware of the man's cheeky smile even as she avoided making eye contact with him. "Rockin' Around the Christmas Tree" played from the diner's overhead speakers, and the smells of bacon and fresh coffee rushed at them as they entered. Addy's stomach growled again at the sight of pancakes and fresh strawberries on a nearby table.

A waitress, with the name Becky stitched on her uniform, quickly seated them.

Addy wasted no time turning the conversation back to Ben once they were alone with the menus.

"What do *you* think of Ben?"

"I think you're right. But we need leverage if we want to get him to tell us what he's hiding."

She felt the beginnings of a headache coming on. "What kind of leverage?"

"Something that would prove he's lying or at least strongly suggest it."

"That makes sense." Addy looked at him inquisitively. "How would you get that kind of evidence?"

Shawn smiled devilishly. "There are many ways, but in this case, I'd start with talking to Cassie's roommate, Suri."

"Suri? Why?"

"Both Ben and Suri told the sheriff that Cassie had moved. That suggests that they either believed that or they coordinated their stories."

Addy nodded slowly, digesting what he'd said.

Becky returned with a pot of coffee and two cups. She set the cups on the table and poured.

"When I didn't hear from Cassie for three days, I called Suri. She didn't know much, and she hasn't responded to any of my subsequent calls," Addy said, breathing in the coffee smell.

"If you're talking about Suri Bedingfield, she moved out of town about a week ago."

"You know her?" Addy turned her surprised eyes on the waitress.

"There may be a bunch of Suris in Hollywood, but not in Bentham. Suri waited tables for me. Left a message on the restaurant's voice mail last Tuesday saying she'd found a job in Garwin and she quit. Worked here for three years. I would have never thought she'd leave me in the lurch like that."

Suri's abrupt departure sounded suspiciously like Cassie's.

Addy and Shawn exchanged a knowing look. "Did Suri say anything else?"

Becky looked at Shawn as if he'd suddenly grown two heads. "What else is there to say after 'I quit'?"

A fair point.

"You ready to order?" Becky set the coffeepot on the table and pulled a pen and pad from her apron pocket.

Addy ordered the Americana breakfast—four pancakes, eggs, toast, bacon and sausage.

She ignored Shawn's wince when she asked Becky for a side order of home fries.

"I'll just have a fruit cup," Shawn said.

Addy grinned as the waitress walked away from the table.

Shawn quirked an eyebrow. "What? You're laughing at me when you ordered enough food to feed a small army."

"I spent the first twelve years of my life on a ranch. I guess the hearty meals stuck with me," Addy said, adding cream and sugar to her coffee and noting that Shawn took his black.

Shawn sipped his coffee. "A ranch, huh?"

"Yeah. My mom's parents owned a small ranch in Texas." Addy smiled as memories of her grandparents, horseback riding and cloudless starry skies flitted through her head. "My parents met when my dad was doing his residency at a hospital in town. He'd grown up in Brooklyn and had every intention of returning as soon as his residency ended."

"Meeting your mom changed his plans, I assume."

"You assume right. My mom couldn't imagine leaving her family or Texas. Dad used to say if Mom had wanted to live on Mars, he would have rented a rocket to get them there. They were madly in love."

"They sound great," Shawn said.

The chatter in the diner ebbed and flowed around them, mixing with the clink of silverware against porcelain cups and plates.

"They were. And I loved growing up in Texas. A year after Cassie was born, Mom was diagnosed with cancer. She was gone a few months later. My dad and grandparents were devastated. My grandmother passed three months after my mother from a broken heart."

Shawn reached across the table for her hand. "I'm so sorry, Addy."

"It was a long time ago. When my grandfather passed a year later, Dad sold the ranch and moved us back to New York so we'd be near his family."

"Making you half city girl, half country girl and totally fascinating," Shawn said, lacing his fingers through hers and looking into her eyes.

She held his gaze, her heart doing a fluttery stutter. An image of holding Shawn's hand as they strolled the Mall in Central Park or took in the view from Belvedere Castle ran through her mind.

Dangerous thoughts for a woman who had sworn off relationships.

She pulled her hand from his and cleared her throat. "Maybe we should talk about our next steps for finding Cassie."

Shawn frowned but leaned back against the

booth and went with the change in subject. "Do you have any ideas?"

"We need to talk to Suri, but she won't answer my calls. We need to figure out how we're going to get her to speak to us," Addy said.

"We'll have to track her down. I'll get someone at West started on that now. What's Suri's last name?"

"Bedingfield," Addy said just as something else popped into her mind. "Hey, why were you so interested in Ben working on the loading docks?"

An expression she couldn't name passed over his face, but before he could answer her, his phone rang.

He looked at the screen. "It's my brother. What's up, Ry?"

Addy turned toward the window and tried not to eavesdrop on Shawn's conversation, an impossible task given there were only a few feet between them.

The familiarity in Shawn's tone coupled with the undercurrent of irritation and a hint of idolization marked the sibling interaction. She wondered if that was what people heard when she and Cassie spoke. And whether she would ever speak to her sister again.

Shawn kept the call brief, but he asked Ryan

to locate contact information for Suri Beding-field.

"Your brother?"

"Yeah." Shawn shifted to put his phone back in his pocket. "He's been a little overbearing."

"About the case you're really in town for?" Addy said with open curiosity.

Shawn made sure no one was near enough to hear them before answering. They were hours after the typical breakfast rush and ahead of the lunch crush. The only other people in the diner were a pair of teenaged girls occupying a table at the other side of the diner. Becky had seated the customers she did have well away from each other. "Yeah. We have a time crunch, and getting a favorable outcome for our client would mean a big boost for our business."

"Yet you offered to help me."

A look she couldn't name crossed Shawn's face for a fleeting moment before disappearing.

The smile that replaced the look was cocky. "I can handle both. I'm that good."

Addy rolled her eyes. She read the cockiness for what it was—a deflection to keep her from asking more questions—but let it go for now.

Becky stopped at their table, plates balanced on her arm. She set Addy's pancakes and eggs in front of her and slid a second plate with toast to a stop. She turned to the waitress that stood behind her and took the plate with a small mountain of bacon and a small bowl from the girl's hands and placed them on the table in front of Addy and Shawn.

"Anything else I can get you, folks?"

Addy had already forked a generously sized bite of pancake in her mouth, so Shawn answered.

"We're good, thanks," he said, humor dancing in his eyes as he watched her eat.

Becky moved away from the table.

"Excuse me," Shawn called out. "Do you know who Suri Bedingfield's new job is with?"

Becky's nose scrunched in thought. "She didn't say a company name or anything in her message, but I just assumed she'd found a better-paying waitressing job over there in Garwin. They got fancier restaurants than we do here, which means bigger tips."

Addy hadn't realized how hungry she was. She finished her food quickly, then rested against the back of the booth.

"Feeling better?" Shawn asked with a raised eyebrow.

"Actually, I am." She looked at his empty bowl. "How can a man your size survive on a wheatgrass muffin and a bowl of fruit?"

"It was a whole-wheat muffin, and egg

whites and spinach are packed with protein. Eating healthy gives me energy."

Addy shook her head, smiling. "I'd rather have bacon." She bit into the piece of bacon in her hand.

Shawn's eyes locked on Addy's. "Well, it doesn't seem to be hurting you any."

A sexy grin turned his lips upward. Her entire body flushed and her heart beat triple time. "I don't recall you being so big a flirt."

He cocked an eyebrow. "I'm stepping up my game since my meager charms didn't hold your attention the last time."

Embarrassment brought heat to her cheeks. "I owe you an apology for ignoring your calls after Ryan's wedding. That weekend was a mistake." She flinched at the hurt expression that crossed his face. "I didn't mean—"

Shawn held up a hand, stopping her. "No, I shouldn't have called you out like that. It was one weekend."

"It was one *incredible* weekend." She pushed her empty plate aside. "It's just, I don't date."

Now both his eyebrows shot up, forming an upside down V over his nose. "Never?"

She shrugged, then rolled her shoulders to relieve some of the tension there. "I have a few friends—just friends," she emphasized, though she wasn't sure why she was explaining all this to him, "I call if I need an escort to a work function or something like that, but since my divorce…" She let her voice trail off.

"I can't imagine what kind of man would let you go." He shifted his gaze to the ceiling as if in thought. "I'm envisioning the world's biggest half-wit. No, half-wit is too many wits. A quarter wit?" He looked at her with a smile tickling his lips. "Or maybe a two-tenths wit."

Addy laughed, as she knew he'd intended.

"No, no. I'm going to go with he's a one-fifth wit," Shawn declared with exaggerated finality.

"Two-tenths is the same as one-fifth," she said with a smile.

"I've never been good at math." Shawn grinned. "But he's definitely short on wits."

"You won't hear me contradicting you, although I'm more than a little biased as I'm the one who got dumped. Or cheated on, to be precise." Addy swallowed the last drops of her now-cold coffee, all traces of humor gone from her voice. "Although to hear Phillip tell it, I drove him to cheat."

Shawn shook his head. "Not possible. You know that, Addy."

She nodded. "I do, but that doesn't mean hearing it from the man you'd planned to spend your life with doesn't affect you."

The muscle on the side of Shawn's jaw jumped and his eyes darkened, but he watched her silently.

For some inexplicable reason, she wanted to tell him about her ex. "Phillip never liked the long hours I worked. I guess when it came down to it, he couldn't stand being the man waiting for his wife to come home."

Shawn shook his head again. "That's a cop-out. I'd consider myself the luckiest man on earth to find myself waiting for you to come home to me."

The surrounding air crackled with unspoken desire.

"Is he why you never returned my calls after our night together?"

"It wasn't about you. You were my first and only one-night stand. I've sworn off relationships."

Whatever response Shawn might have given was forestalled by their waitress's reappearance.

She slapped their check on the table, oblivious to the sexual tension. "Can I get you anything else?"

Addy pushed herself out of the booth. "Excuse me for a minute. I want to, uh, wash my hands."

She wove through the tables to the dimly lit hallway separating the kitchen from the dining area at the rear of the diner and into the ladies' room. She braced her palms against the sink's edge, taking a minute to collect herself after the charged moment with Shawn. She had no idea why she'd told him about her failed marriage, except that some innate instinct told her she could—should—trust him.

Cassie's disappearance had thrown her off-center. She was blowing off work and trusting a man she barely knew. That wasn't exactly true. She knew some parts of him very well.

Addy looked at her reflection in the mirror over the sink. Focus on finding Cassie. And she would, although she didn't think she'd be able to stop her feelings for Shawn deepening with each passing moment they spent together.

She washed her hands and exited the restroom, nearly colliding with a man standing outside the ladies' room door.

A four-inch scar ran along the side of the man's face, combining with sunken eyes and angular cheekbones to give him a menacing, skeletal look.

A shiver ran down Addy's spine. She averted her gaze. "Excuse me." She put as much room as possible between them as she attempted to move past the man.

"You ought to take those fancy manners and go back to New York City," Scarface hissed. "You won't find what you're looking for here."

A wave of fear rolled through her, but she straightened to her full five-foot-eight height and met the man's ugly glare. "Back off."

"It's you who better back off if you know what's good for you." Scarface took a threatening step forward, and Addy moved two steps back.

"Who are you?"

"Wouldn't want you to disappear, too, now, would we?"

Fear turned to fury in an instant. *Too.* Did that mean Scarface knew where Cassie was?

The man took another step forward, filling the space between them.

In the next instant, Scarface spun away from Addy, his back slamming against the wall on the opposite side of the corridor. Shawn put his large frame between Addy and the man.

"Was that a threat against the lady?" Shawn wasn't touching the other man now, but his hands were fisted in front of him, his body taut and ready to strike.

"Not a threat. Just an observation." A scowl twisted the man's face, making it even more grotesque.

"Well, since you seem to be in a sharing

mood, why don't you tell us what you know about Cassie Williams's disappearance," Shawn said.

"I ain't telling you nothing." The man pushed off the wall, ready to strike.

"What's going on back here? Half my customers are standing in this hallway." Becky stopped at the mouth of the corridor. Her eyes fell on the man, and her expression turned to one of disdain. "Teddy Arbury. Why am I not surprised? I warned you about coming in here with your trouble." Becky's fist landed on her hip.

"I ain't the one making trouble, Becky. I'm just trying to use the facilities."

Becky's expression screamed disbelief. "Well, go on, then. Get out of here," she said, her chin jutting toward the men's room.

Teddy shot Shawn a dark look. Teddy slid by, purposely walking closer to Addy than was necessary. Shawn growled a warning as Teddy pushed through the door into the men's room.

"Are you okay?" Shawn asked. He put his arm around Addy's shoulders, pulling her close and leading her toward the diner's doors.

"I'm fine. He didn't touch me. Just caught me off guard," Addy said, soaking in the warmth from his body. "We need to pay."

"I settled the bill already."

"You didn't have to do that. I ate twice as much as you did."

The corners of Shawn's mouth turned up ever so slightly. "More like four times as much."

She reached into her purse for her wallet, but he waved her off. "Don't worry about it. Let's hurry. I want to see where Teddy goes when he leaves."

Chapter Seven

Addy went over the encounter with Teddy in her head as she and Shawn crossed the street to the public surface lot where he'd parked the Yukon. They'd just closed the doors when Teddy lumbered out the diner doors. He turned in the opposite direction from the parking lot where they sat and headed down the sidewalk.

Shawn put the car in gear and followed.

Teddy made a left at the corner and mounted a black motorcycle. He tore off down the street.

"Make sure your seat belt is fastened tight. I'm not sure how long I'll be able to follow him without him realizing it. Yukons aren't exactly commonplace around here."

She'd seen lots of SUVs, but more of the soccer mom variety, with lots of space for kids, dogs and gear. There were very few of the massive SUVs of the kind Shawn drove.

He wasn't wrong about Teddy catching on to the tail. They'd gone about five blocks when the motorcycle made a sudden hard left, crossing over two lanes of traffic and nearly sideswiping a parked car. Shawn couldn't follow.

"Damn." Shawn hit the steering wheel with the palm of his hand.

"We have to go back and find him. I think he knows where Cassie is."

"He'll be long gone before I can turn around in this traffic."

Shawn continued to drive with the flow of traffic. She felt like crying out in frustration. Her phone rang from inside her purse.

Addy accepted the call without looking at the screen, expecting to hear Jarod's irate twang. At last check he'd sent her half a dozen emails, mostly to remind her of things she'd already taken care of.

Instead, the voice on the other end of the line was much more familiar and welcome.

"Addy?" Cassie's tear-streaked voice came from the other end of the phone.

Addy's heart raced at the sound of Cassie's thready voice. "Cassie? Oh my God, Cassie, are you okay?"

Shawn cut across a lane of traffic, drawing an angry honk from a red sedan, and threw the car into Park at the side of the road. He motioned for Addy to put the call on speaker.

She pressed the microphone icon on her

screen and held the phone between her and Shawn. Static crackled from the phone.

"My shoulder...okay, though, I think." The line dropped in and out as Cassie spoke.

"Cassie, where are you?" Addy's heart pounded loudly in her ears. The only response was the sound of static. "Are you there? Cassie?"

"Here... Woods..." Cassie's voice came in a ragged burst between static. It almost sounded as if she were running as she spoke.

Shawn leaned in close and spoke into the phone. "Cassie, my name is Shawn West. I'm helping your sister find you. Can you see anything around you?"

"Not sure..."

The line went silent, Cassie's voice and the static both gone, followed by the telltale beeping that showed the call had dropped.

"Cassie!" Addy cried, the panic in her voice sucking the air from the interior of the car.

She pressed the speaker icon and brought the phone to her ear, hoping that the move might somehow bring her sister back.

Shawn took the phone from her hand, navigating to the recent calls list and hitting redial.

They listened to it ring for thirty seconds before the line went dead again without being picked up or rolling over to voice mail.

Addy gripped Shawn's arm. "We need to go

to the sheriff, right now. Maybe he can trace the call or something."

Shawn nodded, putting the Yukon in gear and getting them to the sheriff's office fifteen minutes later. She and Shawn showed the deputy at the desk their IDs and explained that they didn't have an appointment with the sheriff but that they needed to see him. The deputy hesitated but lifted the receiver of the phone on his desk after several seconds and punched four buttons.

He spoke too softly for Addy to hear what he said through the Plexiglas and over the chatter coming from the people sitting behind her in the waiting area.

The aftershocks of emotion from Cassie's call still vibrated through her.

If Shawn was as impatient to speak with the sheriff, he was better at hiding it. Still, his shoulders were taut. And the assessing sweep of his eyes over the lobby and the officers behind the Plexiglas screen screamed that he was on guard.

The deputy put down the phone, pushing a sign-in sheet and pen through the slit in the glass. They signed in, and less than a minute later the locks on the door to their right clicked and another uniformed deputy waved them through.

Sheriff Donovan looked up from the file he was reading as they entered.

"Ms. Williams. Mr. West. To what do I owe this pleasure?" Donovan's tone conveyed the opposite of his words; he found no pleasure in their reappearance in his office.

Since she was in no way happy to be in his office and the sheriff's cavalier attitude toward Cassie's disappearance may have put her sister in danger, Addy didn't hesitate to engage.

"I just got a call from Cassie. She's being held by someone, possibly in a wooded area." She'd marched from the door to his desk while she spoke, stopping on the visitor's side of the desk and staring down at the sheriff, her hands balled into fists at her side.

"Hold on a minute." Sheriff Donovan pushed back from the desk, raising his hands. "Why don't you have a seat and tell me about this call?"

Shawn stepped up next to her but seemed to understand that this was a fight she wanted to wage by herself. He kept quiet. "I don't want to have a seat, and I just told you about the call. What are you going to do to find out where my sister is being held?"

Sheriff Donovan stood, forcing her to crane her head up to look at his face. "Have a seat,

Ms. Williams." The sheriff gestured to the chairs behind her, his voice and eyes hard.

Neither she nor Sheriff Donovan moved.

Somewhere in the back of her mind, she understood this wasn't a test of wills she could win. She needed the sheriff more than he needed her if she had a hope of finding Cassie. Sheriff Donovan had made it clear that it would suit him just fine if she went back to New York City and let him handle Cassie's disappearance the way he saw fit. If she wanted him to do more than wait and see if Cassie turned up, she might have to try to win him over with honey rather than vinegar.

Possibly thinking along the same lines, Shawn said softly, "Addy, you should sit."

After several seconds, she relented. Shawn took the second chair, while Sheriff Donovan also sat.

"Now tell me about this call." Sheriff Donovan eyed her from across the desk.

Addy recounted the call in detail. It wasn't difficult. Every word of the short conversation was burned into her memory.

"With your permission, I can try to see if the phone company can attach a name or location to the number your sister called from," the sheriff said, digging through a pile of papers on his desk and handing a sheet across to Addy.

A consent form allowing the department to request her records from the telephone company.

"That's it?" Addy asked, looking up from the form in her hand.

"I know you don't want to hear this, but there's nothing more I can do. Not without a location, and it doesn't sound like your sister gave you one."

Addy slid to the edge of her seat. Shawn reached out, taking her hand as if he feared she might launch herself at the sheriff. Frenetic energy coursed through Addy, making launching herself at the sheriff possible, although she held herself in check. She couldn't seem to make the sheriff understand the danger she knew Cassie was in.

"Maybe she couldn't tell us, but the call proves she's being held against her will."

Sheriff Donovan shook his head, sending a thick strand of gray hair onto his forehead. "Maybe."

Addy felt her ire rise to near boiling, but she checked it for Cassie's sake. "What do you mean, maybe?"

"Kidnappers don't usually let their victims make phone calls to family, despite what you see on television. You said the call was choppy. And that your sister said she was okay when you asked how she was. Maybe you just had a bad connection."

"Sheriff—" Addy started, but Sheriff Donovan held up a hand.

"Look, I understand your concern. I do. But there isn't much we can do right now. If your sister called once, she'll probably call again. You may have a better connection next time." Sheriff Donovan stood, crossing his arms over his chest.

Shawn also rose, still holding Addy's hand and pulling her up with him.

"That she called is a good sign, Ms. Williams." The sheriff's gaze cut to Shawn and held some silent communication Addy didn't understand.

Addy started to ask about it when Shawn spoke.

"Let's go, Addy." He moved his hand to her back and guided her out of the sheriff's office.

Addy signed the consent form to allow the sheriff to have her phone records and left it with the deputy at the front desk on the way out. She and Shawn crossed the small parking lot behind the sheriff's office. A light snow fell, and people hustled past the sheriff's department laden with shopping bags. A Salvation Army volunteer stood on the corner across the street, his rhythmic bell enticing passersby to drop change in his red kettle.

Addy hoisted herself into the Yukon, closed the door and turned so she faced Shawn across the middle console. "What was that back there between you and Sheriff Donovan at the end? What did he mean that Cassie's calling was a good sign?"

Shawn took her hand, looking at her with compassion. "It's a good sign because it means Cassie is still alive."

They made their way out of the parking lot, but the words Shawn hadn't said hung thick in the air. Cassie was alive.

But for how much longer?

Chapter Eight

Addy sank into the Yukon's heated leather seats and let her eyes drift closed. She and Shawn had spoken to two of the three people on her list, but it felt like they were no closer to finding Cassie. The call from Cassie had left Addy feeling even more fearful that they were running out of time.

Shawn hadn't yet started the car's engine. She felt him shift in the driver's seat and opened her eyes.

He pulled a bottle of aspirin from the console between them and offered it to her.

"Thanks." The smile she gave him was genuine, albeit weak.

She swallowed two capsules dry. Her mild headache had turned into a raging inferno somewhere between the confrontation with Teddy and their chat with Sheriff Donovan.

Shawn gave her hand a comforting squeeze before hitting a button on the steering wheel.

"Call Ryan."

The sound of a phone ringing came through the car radio's speakers.

"Shawn." The gruff tenor floated through the car.

Shawn turned his gaze on Addy, taking her hand in his again. "You're on speaker, Ry. Addy's in the car with me."

"I'm sorry your sister is missing." The gruff voice on the other end of the phone softened. "West Security will do our best to locate her."

"Thank you. And please call me Addy."

"Addy got a call from Cassie about forty minutes ago. It was short, and the connection was bad," Shawn said.

Ryan asked for her phone and which carrier she used. "I'll see what I can do, but it will take some time."

"There's something else. Before Cassie's phone call, a guy named Teddy Arbury threatened Addy." Shawn quickly recapped the scene at the diner and following Teddy's motorcycle. "I tried to follow him, but he got away from me," Shawn said, his jaw clenching.

"Given how you drive, I'd love to know how that happened," Ryan grumbled.

They could hear Ryan already typing furiously.

Shawn ignored the brotherly dig. "Arbury was riding a black Fireblade."

"Ah, that makes sense. Those bikes are fast."

"Let's see what we can find on him. Also, Cassie's roommate, Suri Bedingfield, seems to have suddenly moved out of their apartment and gotten a new job in Garwin."

"I'm on it. Anything else?" Ryan stressed the last two words.

Irritation flashed across Shawn's face. His jaw clenched tighter. "I'll keep you posted."

The silence on the other end of the phone went on for so long Addy began to wonder if they'd lost the connection.

Finally, Ryan spoke. "I'll be in touch."

Ryan disconnected.

Addy let out a deep breath. "So where to now?"

Shawn started the Yukon. "Let's go check out Cassie's apartment."

They made a quick detour to the office of the real estate agent who'd helped Cassie find her apartment. The agent hesitated to give Addy the spare key until Addy pointed out that she was technically a lessee since the landlord had insisted Addy be the signatory on the lease given Cassie's age and lack of rental history. The agent glowered but handed over the key.

Cassie lived in a yellow clapboard duplex

in a residential area of the city. The cold air slammed into Addy the moment she stepped from the warm interior of the Yukon. Her eyes scanned the small, desolate front yard. The tufts of grass that had survived the winter weather were yellowed and crunched beneath their feet as they made their way to the front of the duplex.

A thought tickled at the back of Addy's mind, but she couldn't bring it into focus.

"You okay?" Shawn gazed down at her, concern in his eyes.

She smiled weakly, mustering a nod.

They climbed the steep, narrow staircase to the second-floor apartment, and Addy used the key to let them inside.

The apartment was small for one person. Having to share it with a roommate would have driven Addy insane. But Cassie had insisted on getting a roommate and paying her way, despite Addy's offers of financial help.

The apartment was freezing, but a musty smell still managed to linger in the air. The paisley sofa and armchair that had come with the furnished apartment remained, but it appeared Suri or Cassie had attempted to add some warmth to desolate space with cherry-red curtains over the living room and kitchen windows and a painting of a boat out to sea on the wall behind the sofa. Along the far wall of the space, three feet of countertop sat between an ancient range stove and an equally old refrigerator. The two cabinets overhanging the counter provided the only cupboard space. There was no dining table, and no room for one. Cassie and Suri must have eaten their meals on the sofa or in their bedrooms.

"Do you know which room was Cassie's?" Shawn asked, peeking into the room that opened up off the living room.

"Since it was her apartment, Cassie took the *slightly*—" Addy emphasized the word "—bigger room with a little more privacy."

Addy pointed and led the way down a short hallway to the second bedroom.

The room looked as if it had been stripped, possibly by someone moving out. An undressed mattress and box spring sat on a metal frame, an upright pine dresser across from it. The closet door stood open, several empty hangers dangling from the closet rod.

There were still months left on the lease, but from all appearances, the apartment looked to have been abandoned by its occupants.

Shawn searched the nightstand next to the bed while Addy explored the dresser, opening each drawer. Nothing. There wasn't so much as a sock in any of them. She reached inside the closet, pushing to her tippy toes, and fanned her hand over the top shelf, feeling for anything that might give her some clue as to Cassie's whereabouts.

Despite her five-foot-eight height, she wasn't quite able to reach the back wall of the closet. Not wanting to miss any potential clue, she dropped back to her heels and rotated in a slow circle, looking for something she could stand on and see into the top of the closet.

On his knees, Shawn peered under the bed. Addy tilted her head, admiring how his jeans hugged his bottom. She wouldn't have thought it was possible for his tush to look better than it had in yesterday's tailored slacks, but the jeans were giving the slacks a run for their money. The man had a killer body.

Shawn turned, catching her off guard. Heat rose in her cheeks and flamed as a slow smile spread across Shawn's face. "What are you doing?"

"I can't reach all the way to the back of the closet. I'm looking for something to stand on." She ignored the pull to fan her cheeks, instead pointing to the nightstand he'd just searched. "Can you help me push that over here?"

Instead of helping her push the nightstand, he wrapped his arms around it and lifted it as if it was no heavier than a stapler.

"Where do you want it?" His flirty smile sent a tingle through her.

"Show-off."

He winked and wiggled his biceps in answer.

Another tingle, this time accompanied by flutters in her stomach and lower. She didn't usually find cocky self-assuredness attractive, but on Shawn? Majorly. Hot.

"Just put it in front of the closet. Thanks."

Shawn set the end table down and reached for her waist as if to hoist her to the top of the table, but she stepped back.

"I think I can manage."

He raised his hands in front of him and took a step back.

She braced a hand on either side of the nightstand and hoisted herself on top, knees first. The table wobbled at the addition of her weight.

Shawn's hand shot out, wrapping around her forearm and steadying her. His lips were only inches from hers. All she had to do was lean in an inch. Her heart pounded.

"This thing is a piece of junk. Take a look, and let's get you off it before it falls apart."

She swallowed hard and nodded, her heart still pounding. She needed to tamp down her libido before she spontaneously combusted.

Shawn held on to her arm as she pushed to her feet and peered into the closet.

Disappointment joined the flutters in her stomach at the sight of the dusty but otherwise empty self.

"See anything?" Shawn asked.

"No."

A cracking sound punctuated the statement. Shawn wrapped his arms around her, swinging her away from the closet. The nightstand crashed to the floor, and one of the legs rolled into the wall with a thunk.

Shawn made no move to put her down. His face flushed with desire and something else that she wasn't sure she was ready to name. She put it aside and did the thing she'd wanted to do since she opened the door to her hotel room and found him standing there this morning.

She reached her arms around his neck and pulled him into a kiss. Shawn's mouth moved against hers without hesitation. The touch of his tongue finally ignited a fire inside her, and all she could think about was how right it felt to be in his arms. He was strong and solid. Confident, cocky even, but kind. For the first time, she let herself consider what it might be like to come home to him and be kissed like this for the rest of her life.

That thought had her breaking off the kiss abruptly. It was one kiss. An admittedly amazing kiss, she corrected mentally, but not a reason to consider changing her life. She had a plan. Find Cassie. Close the Browning–Tuffs merger. Make partner. A relationship just didn't fit into that plan.

"I think you can put me down now."

Confusion clouded Shawn's eyes, but he lowered her to the ground.

"We should check out the rest of the apartment." Addy smoothed her wrinkled shirt and shifted past Shawn and out of the bedroom, avoiding looking him in the eye.

If he had any thoughts about her abrupt change in attitude, he kept them to himself. It was unfair to have kissed him like that when she had no intention of letting anything between them blossom. Maybe she should apologize. But with one glance at the hardened features of his face, she knew that an apology would not go over well right now.

She sighed to herself. He was angry with her, and she deserved it for leading him on. It was something she'd have to deal with. Later.

Addy made her way to the kitchen, Shawn trailing behind her and detouring at the end of the hall into the smaller bedroom that had been Suri's. She opened the refrigerator. Empty. She hadn't expected to find anything inside, but the cool air was a welcome respite from the flames heating her body. She moved to the range and opened the oven door, once again unsurprised when she found it empty.

Addy was the cook in the family, finding it calming and satisfying to start with nothing but raw ingredients and transform them into something that she could share with her friends and family. She doubted Cassie had ever turned on the oven, but that made it the perfect hiding place.

She finished her search of the small kitchen with the cupboards, which held the plates, cups and pots that had come with the apartment. The cabinet drawers were similarly appointed, holding only silverware.

"There's nothing in there," Shawn said, exiting the second bedroom.

"Nothing here, either," Addy responded, frustration ringing from each word. "I guess we can get out of here."

Shawn lifted the ruffled sofa skirt and looked underneath. This time she made a point of not looking at him as he did.

Shawn stood and went to the middle of the room. His eyes passed over her, then stopped just to her right. He crossed to the small kitchen space, his eyes fixed on a point on the ceiling.

"There's an attic or crawl space up there." He pointed to a square cutout in the ceiling. A short string dangled from a hook on one side.

Shawn jumped, grabbing the string. The door swung down. A set of folding stairs had been attached to the inside, and Shawn unfolded them.

Addy stepped forward, ready to ascend the ladder and see what, if anything, was up there. She doubted very much Cassie would have stored anything inside, but she wasn't leaving the apartment without searching every inch of the space.

Shawn held out a hand, blocking her forward movement. "You should let me do it. We don't know how sturdy this old ladder is or what we'll find up there."

Tension rolled off him, and Addy understood what Shawn had not said. He was worried about finding Cassie's body in the attic.

Shawn reached around his back, drawing a gun from his waistband.

He climbed the ladder, gun held in front of him with one hand, the other steadying him as he climbed. He stopped slightly more than halfway up, twisting so he could see behind him and sweeping the gun from left to right.

"There's something up here." He returned the gun to his waistband at his back, signaling that whatever was in the attic wasn't a threat.

Her heart thudded at the possibility that

the worst had happened and they'd just found Cassie.

Shawn climbed farther up the ladder, disappearing inside the attic. After a couple of minutes his head appeared. "Stand back."

A dark gray garbage bag landed at Addy's feet, followed by a second garbage bag moments later.

She knelt, opening a bag as Shawn made his way back down the ladder slowly, a box in his hands.

The trash bags contained women's clothes—jeans, tops, suits, skirts. Addy pulled a faded pink T-shirt from the pile.

"These are Cassie's clothes," Addy said, rooting around in the bags, finding more familiar pieces of clothing.

"And this box looks like it's full of some of her other things." Shawn lifted a sterling silver picture frame from the box open in front of him. Cassie, Addy and their father at Cassie's high school graduation.

Addy came to kneel next to Shawn, taking the picture from his hands. "Cassie would have never moved without taking this photograph with her."

Addy looked from the photo to Shawn, fear lassoing her heart.

"I think you're right. There are other things

in here that I don't think she would have left behind."

Addy scrutinized the objects in the box. A journal with brightly colored swirls on its face. A cell phone charger, although the cell phone appeared to be absent. Cassie's comb, brush and several other grooming implements. All things that she'd have taken with her if she'd been moving back to New York or anywhere.

"I think we have to call Sheriff Donovan," Shawn said, standing. He reached a hand down to her.

She took his hand and let him help her up. "You think he's going to care? He's dug in on the Cassie-moved-away theory."

"He doesn't have much choice but to care. This stuff directly contradicts that theory." Shawn waved his hand over Cassie's belongings.

Addy wasn't so sure of that. Sheriff Donovan had had days to search the apartment and discover this stuff, and he hadn't. Prior experience with men like the sheriff told her that he'd most likely see their discovery as an encroachment on his authority, a sign that they didn't think he'd done his job, which he hadn't.

The sound of footsteps on the stairs outside the apartment drew both their attention before she could voice her concerns. The window in the living room faced the side of the adjacent building while the one in the kitchen looked out onto the small patch of grass at the back of the building. None of the windows in the apartment faced the front, where a visitor was most likely to park, which meant the occupants had no idea who was coming up the stairs.

Shawn reached behind his back for his gun with one hand and gave her a little push toward the hallway with the other. "Get into Cassie's bedroom and lock the door."

Addy moved to the hall but didn't go as far as Cassie's room. She pulled her phone from her back pocket, ready to dial for help.

A fist pounded on the door. "Sheriff. Open up."

Shawn peered out of the small keyhole in the door, his gun still in his hand. "It's Sheriff Donovan."

Addy let out the breath she'd been holding and put her phone in her pocket.

Shawn tucked his gun into the waistband of his jeans and opened the apartment door.

Sheriff Donovan's eyes landed on Shawn, and he grimaced. "What are you doing here? You're trespassing."

"We're doing no such thing," Addy said, moving to Ryan's side. "I'm the cosigner on the lease to this apartment, and I have a key."

She pulled the key from her pocket and held it up for the sheriff to see.

"We were just about to call you, Donovan." Shawn swung the door open wide, stepping aside to let the sheriff in.

The lawman's expression was doubtful as he stepped inside the apartment. "You were? Why?"

"Addy and I took a look around to see if Cassie left any clue as to where she was going. We found something."

The sheriff's gaze narrowed, moving between Addy and Shawn. "Suri Bedingfield let me search this place when you made the initial missing-person complaint, Ms. Williams. All your sister's belongings were gone."

Addy planted her fists on her hips, fury swelling. "Maybe that's because you didn't look well enough." Donovan's eyes glinted darkly, but she didn't care. "We found my sister's clothes and personal items in the attic above the kitchen." She pointed.

"You were with Ms. Williams when she found these things?" Sheriff Donovan's gaze swung in Shawn's direction as if her word alone wasn't sufficient.

"Yes," Shawn responded calmly.

"Did you look in the attic when you did your search?" Addy demanded.

Sheriff Donovan glanced at the bags and box on the floor. "There was no reason to climb up there. Your sister's roommate claimed she'd moved out. Why shouldn't I have believed her?"

"Because I'm her sister, and I told you Cassie wouldn't have left town without telling me about it first." She struggled to keep her anger in check, knowing that yelling at the sheriff wasn't going to help her case with him. Still, her words came out louder than she'd planned.

"Look, Ms. Williams, we can't go chasing down every grown woman that up and leaves town."

Her frustration with the sheriff neared the tipping point.

Shawn's hand came down around her shoulders, and he spoke before she did. "Well, now you have evidence that suggests Cassie didn't just leave of her own will. Or are you suggesting she intended to move back to New York but left personal effects like her graduation picture and journal behind?"

Sheriff Donovan looked as if he wanted to argue the point, but thought better of it. "I'll have one of my deputies come process those things for evidence. But I need you two out of here before you compromise the scene any further."

That was the last straw. Donovan hadn't done

his job, so she'd had to do it for him, and he had the nerve to suggest that she'd compromised Cassie's missing-person case.

Addy stepped toward the sheriff, aware of his hand going to the butt of his weapon as she did, but too angry to stop herself from speaking. "If we hadn't come here and searched—"

Shawn reached for her hand, drawing her back toward him. "You'll let us know what you find, Sheriff," he said a little too loudly, cutting her off.

The sheriff didn't answer, just jerked his head toward the door.

Shawn pulled her from the apartment, his back never turned completely to the sheriff.

At the bottom of the steps, he turned to her, his mouth turned down in a frown. "You need to be more careful around Donovan."

"Don't you start with me." She was in no mood for a lecture, but the trembles rolling through her body weren't just anger. The import of what could easily have happened hit her. She marched to the Yukon.

"You have been Black in America your entire life, correct?"

"I. Said. Don't. Start." She grabbed the car's door handle and pulled. The door didn't budge.

She rested her forehead against the passenger window, unsure if she could have hoisted herself into the car if she'd gotten the door open. The adrenaline and rage high she'd been on when she'd confronted the sheriff receded, leaving nothing but the fear that she would never see Cassie again.

"I'm sorry. I know getting into it with the sheriff was stupid. I just…" A sob escaped at the same time the tears began rolling down her face.

Shawn wrapped his arms around her, cradling her into his chest.

The fear and concern she'd been holding inside for days erupted like a volcano. She couldn't stop it and instead gave in to it, holding on to Shawn like he was her lifeline, because for those few minutes he was the only thing holding her together.

After several minutes, she drew back out of his arms. "I'm sorry." She swiped at her eyes.

"Don't be. If the situation were reversed and one of my brothers was missing, I would have fallen apart a long time ago. Even if it was Ryan."

She let the ends of her mouth turn up at his paltry attempt at a joke.

"Let's get out of here." He beeped the car unlocked.

Addy slid to the side to let him open the passenger door for her. Propping a foot on the running board, she pulled herself into the car.

Shawn didn't immediately close the door, his attention focused on the front right tire. "Damn it."

He shut the door and the car beeped, an indication that he'd locked her inside.

She leaned forward in the leather seat, watching as Shawn crouched by the tire, running his hand over the thick rubber before moving around the front of the car and examining the tire there before getting in the car.

"What's wrong?"

"Someone punctured both the front tires."

Addy glanced back at the door to the duplex. "Sheriff Donovan?"

"We can't prove it," Shawn said, shooting a glance at the sheriff's nearby SUV.

The sheriff had parked his cruiser next to the Yukon. It would have been easy for him to slash the car's tires before heading inside. It probably wouldn't have taken more than half a minute to puncture both.

Shawn started the car. "All of West's vehicles have run-flat tires. I'll have to get new ones today, but I want to get us out of here right now."

"You think the sheriff wants to keep us here

for a particular reason?" Addy asked, her heart jumping into her throat.

If the sheriff intended to hurt them, she'd nearly given him an excuse inside.

Shawn put the Yukon in gear and backed out of the parking space. His eyes met hers as the car rolled forward. "I don't know, but we aren't going to stick around to find out."

Chapter Nine

Shawn drove them back to the hotel and made a call to roadside assistance. A tech arrived within the hour and quickly changed the tires on the Yukon. Addy retreated to the bedroom in the suite.

She'd planned to get a quick nap, but her brain wouldn't shut down long enough to allow sleep to come.

Someone had put Cassie's things in that attic, most likely to make it look like Cassie had left town. As Cassie's boyfriend, Ben was a prime suspect, and his nervousness this morning added to Addy's suspicion of him. But Ben wasn't the only suspicious actor here.

Suri was missing in action. She still hadn't returned Addy's call. According to Sheriff Donovan, Suri had also reported that Cassie had moved back to New York. But it seemed unlikely that all Cassie's clothes and personal items would have made it into the attic without Suri knowing anything about it. Cassie and Suri had only met after Cassie placed an ad for a roommate with an online home-share company. The company had conducted background checks on both Suri and Cassie as part of their policy and Suri's had come back clean, but what did that mean, really? She was glad Shawn had thought to have his brother check into Suri. She had no doubt West would be far more thorough than the home-share company.

Addy's stomach clenched at the thought that Cassie might have been sharing a home with someone out to get her.

Addy's phone beeped a notification that she had a new voice mail. She listened as Jarod fumed about her needing to get back to the office now. As he fulminated, she scrolled through her emails, finding that Jarod had sent several new ones in the last couple hours.

She exited voice mail and dashed off a hasty email reassuring Jarod that she had things under control. She swung her legs over the side. The thought that had been floating just out of reach when she and Shawn arrived at Cassie's apartment crystallized.

She crossed the bedroom and opened the door.

Shawn looked up from the computer in his lap. "Have a good nap?"

"I couldn't sleep. I just kept wondering what it means that we found Cassie's stuff and still no Cassie."

"We're doing everything we can. We'll find her." The determination in his voice reassured her.

"What are you doing?" Addy crossed the room.

Shawn tapped several keys as she sat beside him. "Ryan sent the background checks I asked for on Ben and Suri."

"Yeah? Anything interesting?" She leaned into him, trying to see his screen, but the reflective coating over it made that impossible.

"Here. You won't be able to see it unless you're looking at it head-on." He shifted the laptop from his lap to hers.

The report on screen had Suri Bedingfield's name on top, followed by her birth date, place of birth and other personal information.

"The interesting stuff is on the third page. Ry was able to get a current address in Garwin, but what's more interesting is that she's living in a condo that rents for fifteen hundred dollars a month."

Addy felt her eyes go wide. "How in the world?"

"How much was rent on the duplex?"

"Just under nine hundred a month."

Shawn laced his fingers behind his head. "So Suri went from paying four fifty a month in rent to over a thousand? And her new job. It's not in food service." Shawn leaned forward, pointing to an area at the bottom of the screen. "She's working as an office manager for a sprinkler manufacturer."

"How? Becky said Suri worked for her since she'd dropped out of high school. Why would this company hire her to manage their office with no management experience?"

"That's an excellent question," Shawn said but offered no answer.

A myriad of thoughts collided in Addy's mind. "Part of the reason I couldn't get any sleep was thinking about whether Suri could have had a hand in Cassie's disappearance." Addy waved a hand at the computer screen. "This, none of this, makes any sense."

"I think we should take a ride to Garwin tomorrow."

"Can't we go tonight?"

Shawn ran a hand over the shadow of stubble on his jaw. "I can't. I have a meeting I have to go to tonight, and I want to look into Suri a little more before we question her."

Addy crossed her arms. "What about the report on Ben?"

"The associate's degree in business is legit.

He's got a couple pops on his record for marijuana. Using, not selling. I'd bet there are a few more on a sealed juvie record somewhere. But nothing that stands out."

She set the laptop aside and got to her feet. "But the way he acted this morning? And now with finding Cassie's stuff hidden in the apartment. That proves he and Suri were lying about Cassie moving." She fisted her hands on her hips.

"It doesn't prove anything." Shawn stood. He held up a hand. "I'm not saying Donovan and the others are right. But Cassie could have put those things there herself. We have no proof she didn't."

Frustration swelled in Addy's chest. She had to be back in New York in two days, and so far she'd only managed to find more questions and absolutely no answers.

"I remembered what was bothering me at Cassie's apartment. Her scooter is missing."

"Scooter?"

"Cassie bought a little scooter to get to and from work. It wasn't in the apartment's parking lot."

Shawn ran a hand over his head. "We should call Donovan and see if we can get him to put out an APB on the scooter."

Addy frowned. Their last encounter with the

sheriff hadn't gone well. "You really think he'll help us?"

"I don't know, but it can't hurt to ask. After we do that, I want to go talk to Ben again."

She glanced at her watch. "It's quarter after four. If we hurry, we might still catch him at Spectrum. I can call the sheriff on the way."

"Great. Just give me a minute." Shawn rose and disappeared into the bedroom.

She scanned a few more pages in the report on Suri, then moved the mouse to the task bar. The cursor hovered over Ben's report, but the document next to it caught her eye.

She left clicked, bringing up a background report bearing her name.

It contained more information about her than she'd have thought possible for someone outside law enforcement to get—where she lived, worked, even banked. The report contained details of her father's illness and death; even a copy of her divorce settlement appeared as an attachment at the end of the document.

Comment bubbles appeared throughout the document identifying their author as Ryan West. Little notes about one thing or another in her life. She scrolled through them, stopping at a note made in the paragraph highlighting her father's $100,000 life insurance policy and the amount of debt her divorce and her father's illness had left her with.

100k reasons for A to disappear C? Ryan had commented.

A wave of anger rose inside her that turned unexpectedly sharp as she read Shawn's typed response.

Look into who gets the money.

The rational side of her brain attempted to interject reason. One amazing weekend together six months ago didn't give Shawn a reason to trust her. He didn't know her, and when a person went missing it was most often at the hands of those closest to them, right?

Still, she found it hard to be rational. Hurt stabbed her in the chest.

Shawn thought she was capable of hurting Cassie. It felt like a betrayal.

The bathroom door squeaked as it opened.

She minimized the report with her name and brought Suri's back on screen.

"Ready to go?" Shawn asked.

"Yeah, sure." She set the laptop aside and got to her feet.

A crease bloomed above Shawn's brow. "You okay?"

"Fine. We should go before Spectrum closes."

Chapter Ten

The temperature had fallen another ten degrees by the time Shawn and Addy arrived at Spectrum just before five. He'd spoken to Ryan while Addy had attempted to take a nap. Ryan had agreed that finding Cassie's things wasn't a good sign, but he hadn't been ready to let go of the theory that Cassie might be somehow involved in the chip fraud.

He'd given serious thought to coming clean with Addy about the possibility that Cassie's disappearance had something to do with a multimillion-dollar scheme to sell fraudulent computer chips. In the end, obligation to the client won out, and he said nothing.

Not that Addy appeared to want to talk to him. She'd been silent for most of the drive, only speaking in response to a question or statement from him, and only with the briefest of responses.

He'd been around enough women to know

when one was angry, although he couldn't imagine why she'd be angry with him. If anyone should be upset, it should be him.

When she'd kissed him, he'd stupidly allowed himself to think, for just the briefest of seconds, that they might have a chance. But then she'd pulled away like his lips had turned to molten lava and had avoided even looking him in the eye.

The least she could do if he'd done something to upset her was to tell him.

"Something bothering you?" he asked in a clipped tone.

"No, I'm fine," Addy answered without taking her eyes from the scenery passing by outside the car window.

Fine. If she didn't want to talk, they wouldn't talk. He wasn't in any rush to get kicked in the teeth again, anyway.

He parked the Yukon in the same parking lot from that morning, and he and Addy made their way to Spectrum offices.

Unlike earlier that morning, no one sat behind the reception desk.

"That's fortunate. Let's go on back. Maybe we can catch Ben off guard."

They walked side by side, but he made sure to keep a respectable distance between them. Addy stayed in step with him but didn't look his way as they made their way through the corridors of the office.

The floor was emptier than it had been earlier in the day. The door to Ben's office stood open, but it was empty, the lights off. When did this guy work?

"Can you act as a lookout while I search?"

"Lookout? You sound like we're about to pull off a heist," Addy said, the corners of her mouth turning up slightly.

He felt some of the pressure in his chest loosen.

Addy stood near the door while he went to Ben's desk.

He wiggled the mouse next to the desktop computer. The screen came to life, demanding a password.

He turned the keyboard over and searched under the desk. Despite the many high-profile hacking incidents in the past several years, people still did asinine things like taping their passwords to their computers and desks. It appeared Ben wasn't one of those people, but he didn't lock his desk drawers, not that there appeared to be a need for him to. The drawers were empty except for the usual office products— pens, a box of paper clips, a letter opener. In the larger bottom drawer, Shawn found three legal pads, still in the cellophane wrapper. He'd only been in the job a matter of weeks, but it certainly didn't seem like Spectrum had given Ben a ton of responsibility.

Shawn went to his knees and reached upward, running his hand over the underside of the top drawer. He hadn't expected to find anything but wasn't surprised when his hand moved over a small square envelope taped to the underside.

He pulled the envelope free and opened it.

A computer chip with the Intellus logo stamped on it fell into his hand.

"Someone is coming," Addy hissed, stepping away from the office door.

He put the chip back in the envelope and shoved it into his back pocket. Using one hand, he grabbed a square Post-it pad and pen from the desk. He hunched over the desk as if he'd been writing out a note to leave for Ben.

"What are you doing in this office? Who are you?" A slender man with unnaturally bronze skin available only in a tanning salon stopped in Ben's office doorway.

"I'm Addy Williams. I'm Cassie Williams's sister. This is my friend Shawn West."

Shawn straightened, waving the sticky note he'd quickly scrawled in the air. "We were just leaving a note for Ben."

As if a light had been switched on, the man's

frown turned into a smile. "I'm Lance Raupp, vice president of Spectrum Industries."

Lance stretched his hand out to Addy while his eyes swept over her body in obvious examination.

"Martin Raupp's your father?"

Lance's eyes flashed surprise. "Have you met?"

"Earlier today."

Shawn rounded the desk, his jaw tightening in irritation. Lance held on to Addy's hand much longer than was appropriate. Shawn stopped next to Addy, thrusting his hand out.

Lance frowned but dropped Addy's hand and shook Shawn's in a tight grip.

Lance took his hand, smirking as he did so, Shawn's pique and the reason for it apparently not lost on the man.

"We spoke to Ben this morning, and we were hoping to catch him for a few follow-up questions, but it looks like we missed him," Addy said, taking a step closer to Shawn while putting more distance between herself and Lance.

"I'm sure Ben will do whatever he can to help you locate your sister, but I believe he went home early today." Lance turned a charming smile on Addy.

"Maybe you can help, then," Shawn said.

Lance's gaze narrowed on Shawn. "Spectrum is a small company, but I can't say I knew Miss Williams."

"But you were aware she'd gone missing? How is that?" Shawn asked.

"As I said, Spectrum is a small company. Word gets around. I was under the impression Miss Williams moved back to her hometown of New York City." Lance pulled at the cuff of his left sleeve.

"She didn't," Addy said flatly. "We have reason to believe she didn't leave Bentham on her own, if she left town at all."

Lance raised an eyebrow, shooting Addy a curious look. "Really? And what, may I ask, gives rise to this belief?"

"Did Sheriff Donovan interview you?" Shawn asked without acknowledging Lance's question.

Lance gave Shawn a probing look, no doubt an action that had made many a man squirm. Unfortunately for Lance, he was not one of those men. Shawn met the other man's gaze with equal scrutiny.

"No. No doubt he saw no need to do so. Miss Williams was an intern. Caroline Webb, my human resources director, was her supervisor."

"Would you mind if we spoke to Ms. Webb again?"

"I know the sheriff already talked to her, but

I'm sure she'd be happy to speak with you." This time his smile was tight and forced.

"Everyone seems willing to buy into the theory that Cassie just woke up one day and left town. But as you said, she was a solid, dependable worker. Wouldn't she, as a solid, dependable employee, have given notice to her employer?"

"I don't know. I'm sure you know your sister better than I do." Lance turned away from Shawn, sliding another smile at Addy.

Shawn fought the desire to punch the man in the face. Thankfully, Addy didn't seem to be buying Lance's routine.

Her eyes narrowed on Lance. "You're right, I do know my sister. Even if Cassie had decided to move home, she would have given notice. An email or phone call would have only taken minutes."

In the several silent moments that passed, Shawn read the change in Lance. He realized the charming shtick wasn't going to lead to Addy falling all over him. Abandoning it, he adopted what Shawn suspected was a much more natural countenance. Superiority.

Lance glanced at the expensive Rolex on his wrist. He'd schooled his facial features into an expression of boredom.

"I don't know what to tell you," he said while tapping his right foot.

Shawn had spent enough time studying people to know a nervous tic when he saw one.

Lance looked back at Addy, his expression not nearly as friendly as before. "I'm late for a meeting."

"Lance," a voice called from the hall. "Here you are." Martin Raupp appeared at the door to Ben's office. "Oh, Ms. Williams, Mr. West, so nice to see you both again. Has there been any news on Cassie's whereabouts?"

"I'm afraid not," Addy answered.

Martin took both her hands in his. "Please know I am keeping her and you in our nightly prayers."

"Thank you," Addy said.

Shawn's gaze danced between the two Mr. Raupps. Martin Raupp appeared to be genuinely concerned about his missing employee. Unfortunately, the apple seemed to have fallen far from the tree with respect to the man's son.

"Lance, we're late for the meeting with the distributor." Martin's bushy eyebrows rose.

"I'm going to have to ask you to leave Ben's office since he's not here." Lance stepped aside, gesturing for Addy and Shawn to leave the office.

They moved past Lance out of the office, and he snapped the door closed.

Shawn spoke just as both Raupps began walking away. "If you could just remind us of the location of Ms. Webb's office before you go."

Lance did a slow turn, facing Addy and Shawn once again. "I think she's also left for the day. Maybe you can give her a call tomorrow and set up a time that works for all of you." Lance's smile didn't reach his eyes.

The likelihood that all they'd ever get was Ms. Webb's voice mail was one hundred percent.

"That was interesting," Addy said, watching Lance and his father turn the corner at the end of the hall.

"You can say that again. Come on. I've got to get you back to the hotel."

Darkness had descended on the town while they were inside, and the temperature had fallen even farther. They hustled to the Yukon. Neither spoke until they were inside with the heat blasting away the frigid air.

"We need to go see Suri Bedingfield," Addy said as Shawn pulled into late-afternoon traffic. "She and Ben are the ones who said Cassie left town. If we can't find him and make him tell us why they lied, we have to find her and make her tell us."

"Tomorrow morning."

"Tomorrow? Garwin is only a forty-five minute drive."

He shot her a sidelong glance. "I have somewhere I need to be this evening."

"But if we can get Suri to admit she lied about Cassie leaving town, Sheriff Donovan will have to take her disappearance seriously."

"We will. I just can't do it tonight."

"What? I—"

Her phone rang, interrupting whatever she'd planned to say. She scrambled for the purse at her feet, pulling the phone from the outside pocket quickly, her face awash with hope. Her face fell when she saw the screen. "Damn it." He watched her punch the ignore button.

"We'll go to Garwin first thing in the morning and talk to Suri before she leaves for work."

Addy stared out of the passenger side window, saying nothing further. Anger poured off her.

He pulled into a parking space in the hotel's lot and turned to her. "I'm sorry, but I can't miss this meeting." He reached for her hand, and she turned toward him. "It's for the case I'm in town on. This will give you a chance to catch up on work."

Addy pulled her hand back. "No, I under-stand," she said, getting out of the car.

His jaw clenched as he got out of the driver's side and rounded the car. They fell in step next to each other, headed for the hotel entrance.

"Addy, wait."

She marched on. "You've spent most of your time helping me, and I'm grateful, but you have a job to do," Addy said.

The stiffness in her body made it clear she was still upset, but there wasn't anything he could do about it. "First thing tomorrow. I promise."

Shawn got Addy safely ensconced in the suite before heading out again. He felt bad that they couldn't go to Garwin to talk to Suri this evening, but he only had two days until the fraudulent chips were supposed to be delivered. He'd been neglecting the Intellus case.

His first stop was to a twenty-four-hour cou-rier service. He suspected the chip he found in Ben's office was one of the knockoffs, but he needed the computer gurus back at West to make the final determination. The courier service assured him that they could have the chip at West's New York offices by 10:00 p.m. that night.

He dialed the number for West's tech de-partment.

"Sup?" Tansy Carlson answered the phone. He could see her short, spiky pink hair and array of silver lip rings in his mind's eye. Tansy was one of West's best computer technicians. He quickly explained the situation. Long nights and unusual hours weren't out of the ordinary for West's employees, and Tansy assured him she'd be on hand to receive and process the chip as soon as it arrived.

He ended the call and headed to the address for Spectrum's factory.

The factory was located twenty minutes outside town on a street lined with dingy gray warehouses.

Shawn drove around the perimeter of the building. A brass plaque next to the front entrance denoted the factory as a "Carrier-Forest LLC property." He made a mental note to research the LLC when he returned to the hotel and continued to circle the building.

A tall chain-link fence encircled the property. Security cameras pointed at the front and side doors, as well as the doors leading from the building to the loading dock. That didn't mean much. Anyone capable of using Spectrum's distribution line to create fraudulent chips wouldn't have much difficulty getting around the security cameras.

Shawn parked on the street at the far edge of

the factory property, out of sight of the cameras. Workers began trickling out of the employee entrance at exactly five thirty, and by five thirty-five, men and women streamed from the building in pairs and small groups. A young white blond man and a stockier man with dark skin and black hair headed for the far corner of the parking lot.

The blond reached for the door handle on a beat-up red pickup truck with a white-paneled door and called over the top of the truck, "Hey, Jorge. Got time for a drink?"

Jorge pointed his keys at a newer black pickup truck with chrome wheels, beeping it unlocked. "The missus is visiting her sister this week. I'm a free man." Jorge threw his arms open wide and grinned.

The blond laughed as both men got into their respective pickup trucks.

Shawn put the Yukon in gear and followed the trucks a short distance to a sports bar.

Music streamed from overhead speakers, and televisions strategically placed around the restaurant and over the bar beamed various sports events in closed caption.

About half the tables in the dining section were full, and a half dozen people sat scattered around the large bar.

Shawn grabbed a seat two stools down from the Spectrum employees he'd followed.

They'd ordered beers and chatted loudly enough for Shawn to hear their conversation.

Mostly work stuff. He overheard the blond refer to Lance Raupp as a jerk, a determination Shawn couldn't argue with. The stockier guy seemed to prefer to gossip about a coworker's extramarital affair.

The blond guy left to use the washroom, and Shawn turned to Jorge. "You guys work at Spectrum?"

Jorge cut his eyes toward Shawn, a wary look creasing his brow. "Yeah."

"I couldn't help but overhear. Man, I applied for a delivery job weeks ago, but I haven't heard nothin'."

Jorge cocked his head to the side and angled his body so he faced Shawn. "Yeah, it can be hard to get in the door."

"Even harder if you have a record. Did a year and a half for selling dope, only to get out and find out they made the stuff legal?" Shawn twisted his lip into a disgusted sneer that was only partially practiced. It really was messed up how many Black and brown people languished in jail for doing what legislatures in an increasing number of states now made millions of dollars in tax revenue on.

"Yeah, ain't that a trip. I got a cousin in prison right now for selling the same stuff the gringos in Massachusetts are making bank on." Jorge tipped his beer at Shawn. "Different rules for them."

Shawn signaled the bartender for another beer and leaned toward Jorge as if he was about to reveal the secrets of the universe. "The job I applied for, it's loading boxes onto delivery trucks. I've worked for big-time companies like Spectrum before. Not all the guys on the loading docks show up in the company books. You know what I mean?"

The leather-faced bartender slid an open bottle in front of Shawn without stopping, moving to the other end of the bar.

Jorge eyed Shawn, assessing.

Shawn held the man's gaze, waiting for Jorge to decide whether to trust Shawn.

The blond guy returned before Jorge rendered his final judgment.

"Hey, you ready for round two?" The blond clapped a hand on Jorge's shoulder.

"This is Shawn," Jorge said, pointing. "Shawn. Granger. He works with me at Spectrum. Shawn was just asking about working at Spectrum. You know, the kind of work Alvin does sometimes."

Jorge slid a look at Granger.

Granger's bushy blond brows lowered. "We don't know nothing about that. Try human resources."

"No problem." Shawn raised his hands. "If you say Spectrum is a hundred percent legit, it's a hundred percent legit."

Jorge snorted. "I wouldn't say that."

"Jorge."

Jorge waved his friend off. "Spectrum sometimes hires off the books. I'd usually throw the work my cousin's way." Jorge shrugged. "I can't promise anything, but I can let you know if I hear anything."

The blond man scowled and took his beer to the other end of the bar.

"Can't ask for more than that." Shawn jotted his phone number on a napkin and passed it to Jorge.

He shot the breeze with Jorge for a while longer before leaving the bar.

He knew putting off talking to Suri Bedingfield until morning had disappointed Addy, but at least his trip to the bar had been fruitful. If Spectrum used off-the-books labor, they'd most likely use it to move their fraudulent chips. Hopefully, Jorge would call tomorrow with an illicit job offer Shawn would be more than happy to accept.

He stopped off at the diner and picked up a

piece of apple pie as a peace offering to Addy before heading to the hotel.

His phone rang as he exited the Yukon and headed inside. He pressed the button on the speaker hooked around his ear.

"Hey, Ryan. I'm making progress on the case." He spoke before his brother could.

He filled Ryan in on finding the chip with the Intellus logo in Ben's office and the conversation he'd had with Jorge.

"That chip is a good find, but it won't be enough by itself." Ryan voiced Shawn's earlier conclusion.

Shawn stepped off the elevator and headed toward the suite.

"I know. I plan to track down Ben Konstam tomorrow and lean on him hard to get him to talk."

Shawn held his key card against the black box affixed to the room door. Two beeps sounded, and the red dot on the door turned green.

The darkened living room had him dropping the pie to the floor and reaching for the Glock in his waistband before he crossed the room's threshold. It was only eight thirty, far too early for Addy to have gone to bed.

"Addy?" He held his gun low but at the ready.

"What's wrong?" Ryan demanded.

Shawn didn't answer his brother.

He flicked on the lights, taking in every inch of the room in moments. The bedroom door was open.

His heart beat wildly, but he listened past it, ears perked for any sound in the suite.

He moved forward quickly, checking the bathroom and the closet.

The suite was empty.

"Shawn? Talk to me. What's going on?"

He forced the words past the lump that had formed in his throat.

"Addy's gone."

Chapter Eleven

Snow began to fall as Addy left the Bentham town limits, leaving the streets slick and turning the forty-five-minute trip between Bentham and Garwin into an hour-and-a-half drive. Sitting alone in the suite after Shawn left, the sense that she was running out of time to find Cassie had grown until it nearly overwhelmed Addy. She was grateful for his help, but there was no reason she had to wait for him to talk to Suri.

She'd only had a quick glimpse at the Garwin address in the background report West had done on Suri Bedingfield, but she'd remembered it easily.

Skirting the New York–Massachusetts border, Garwin was twice the size of Bentham but still much smaller than New York City. Three decades ago, the city's politicians had successfully courted a midsize pharmaceutical company, which had established its headquarters in Garwin. Other businesses sprouted up to support the influx of new residents, making Garwin an important small city in the area. The Garwin City Council must have used the same holiday decorator as Bentham—strings of white lights twisted around the base of every lamppost, with red-and-green happy-holidays banners as toppers.

Addy found an open parking spot on the busy street in the heart of downtown Garwin, across from a modern glass-and-chrome high-rise. It looked like Shawn was right about Suri's new apartment being an improvement over the duplex she and Cassie had shared.

Addy's phone rang as she exited the Mustang. She didn't need to look at the screen to know the caller was Shawn.

For a brief moment, she contemplated not answering, but she didn't want to worry him unnecessarily. She stopped on the sidewalk next to the car and connected the call. "Hello, Shawn."

"Are you okay? Where are you?" The panic threading his words sent a stab of guilt through her.

"I'm fine. I'm in Garwin on my way to talk to Suri."

Shawn swore. "Have you talked to her yet?"

The wind whistled by, buoyed by the tunnel

created by the high-rise buildings on either side of the street. She pulled her coat tight against the gale. "No. I just got to her apartment. I haven't gone in."

"Good. Don't. We don't know if she had a hand in Cassie's disappearance. She could be dangerous."

"I doubt she's going to do anything to me in her apartment. It's a big building. Lots of neighbors to overhear and a doorman who would notice if I didn't come back down."

"Addy, just wait for me. I can be there in an hour."

She shook her head, dashing behind a white minivan and across the street. "I'll be fine, Shawn. I've got to go."

Addy ended the call before he could argue further and headed toward the apartment building. No point arguing. She was here, and she wasn't going to wait another minute to get answers.

She already felt as if a clock ticked over her head, every passing minute leading her further and further away from finding Cassie. Every fiber of her being screamed that Cassie was still alive, but the same intuition told Addy that Cassie wouldn't remain that way if she wasn't found soon.

She tugged open the heavy glass doors and crossed the white marble–tiled floors to the doorman's station.

A lanky young man in a turban and a doorman's uniform smiled as she approached. "Good evening. May I help you?"

"I'm here to see Suri Bedingfield."

"Your name, ma'am?" the doorman asked, reaching for the phone on his desk.

Addy gave her full name and waited while the phone rang. After several rings, the doorman replaced the receiver in its cradle. "I'm sorry. It seems Miss Bedingfield isn't at home presently. Would you like to leave a message for her?"

Addy looked at the phone still in her hand. A text from Shawn waited, but she ignored it and looked at the time. Fifteen minutes after seven. Suri could just be working late.

"No. No, thank you. I'll try her again later."

She jogged back across the street to her car. Sliding in, she turned the engine back on and cranked up the air. She'd already made the trip; it wouldn't hurt to wait awhile.

She dashed off a text to Shawn while she waited.

S not home yet. Waiting to see if I can catch her.

The number of pedestrians streaming by on the sidewalk diminished considerably as Addy waited for Suri to return home.

Twenty minutes into the wait, with no response from Shawn to her text, the phone rang. She answered without checking the caller ID, fully expecting the person on the other end of the phone to be a furious Shawn. Instead, she got a furious Jarod.

"Addy, finally. We need you back here now," Jarod barked.

Addy bit back a swear. "Jarod, we talked about this. It's Tuesday. I'll be back in time for the meeting on Thursday."

"You said you'd be available, and you haven't been," Jarod snapped. "I'm not confident you're ready for this meeting. The presentation slides are all wrong. They need to be redone, and you need to be in the office tomorrow by nine."

There were nearly sixty associates in the practice group who could rewrite the presentation, which was perfectly fine the way it was. Not to mention Jarod could do more than shake the client's hand and take all the credit if he really felt that more should be done.

She shook her head even though she knew he couldn't see her. "I can't do that. Transfer the project to another senior associate if you feel that's best."

"Transfer," Jarod sputtered. "The clients love you. How do you expect me to explain your absence to them? No, I expect you in the office tomorrow at nine," Jarod said, his tone indicating he expected that to be the final word. Outside, the moon came out from behind a cloud, spraying light across the windshield.

It suddenly became crystal clear to Addy just how much Jarod and the firm would require her to sacrifice to make partner.

Her stomach flip-flopped wildly, but her voice held steady. "I quit."

An SUV swooshed past her parked car, but the other end of the phone line remained silent for several long seconds.

"Addy, think about this," Jarod said in a tone that was softer and far more conciliatory than it had been a moment ago. "You're a year away from making partner. Everything you've worked for. This is about your career here."

"No, Jarod. This is about something more important than my career. This is about finding my sister." She hung up the phone without giving her boss another chance to speak.

Her hands shook.

A voice screamed in her head to call back. Apologize. Smooth things over. But she knew the only way to make things right was to show up at Covington and Baker tomorrow at nine, and that was something she just could not do.

She tucked her phone into the side pocket of her purse and tried to focus on what needed to be done to find Cassie.

Thirty more minutes passed before Addy finally spied Suri strolling down the sidewalk toward the building.

Addy had only met Suri once, when she'd visited Cassie not long after she'd moved to Bentham. She'd been pleasant but standoffish, mostly staying in her room when Addy and Cassie were in the apartment. Then, the slight blonde had worn her hair long and mostly up in a messy bun. Though Suri and Cassie were the same age, Suri looked years older and perpetually tired.

Even from a distance, Addy could see that Suri had undergone a significant makeover. She'd lightened her dark blond hair and cut it into a stylish angled bob. Suri's sleek black suit and strappy heels looked to be designer.

She waited until Suri entered the lobby of her building and disappeared into the elevator before exiting her car a second time. She started around the front of the car and pulled up short as a large dark figure moved in from her right.

Addy yelped, tripping backward over the curb.

A hand shot out, steadying her before she fell. "Take it easy. It's just me."

"Jeez. You scared me. What are you doing here?"

The tic in Shawn's jaw returned. "You took the words right out of my mouth."

"Look, I get you have a paying client to answer to, but my sister could be in serious trouble. I will not wait around while you chase down some cheating husband or whatever."

Shawn's nostrils flared. "That's not fair. I've been right there with you looking for Cassie."

Addy averted her gaze, guilt tripping through her. He was right. He and West Security had gone above and beyond helping her look for Cassie.

She held up a hand. "Look, can we discuss this later? We're both here now, so let's just go talk to Suri."

His jaw twitched, but he stepped to the side, sweeping his arm out in an "after you" gesture.

They crossed the street and entered the lobby of Suri's building.

The doorman smiled anew as Addy approached.

"Would you like me to try Miss Bedingfield again?"

"Yes, please."

This time Suri answered the phone, but from

the doorman's facial expression, she wasn't happy to hear who her visitors were.

Before the doorman could hang up the phone, Addy leaned forward over the top of his high standing desk. "Suri, we found Cassie's things in the attic of the apartment. You can talk to us or you can talk to the police. Your choice."

The doorman's mouth fell open at the mention of the police.

"Let them up," Suri said from the other end of the line.

Shawn and Addy stepped out of the elevator on the tenth floor and headed to Suri's apartment halfway down the hall.

The door swung open at the first knock.

Suri had changed from her work clothes into a pair of cutoff shorts and an Atlantic City tank top. The scowl on her face was a contradiction with her beach-friendly attire.

"I don't know why you're here. I already told Sheriff Donovan everything I know."

"I don't think that's true," Addy said. "Can we come in?"

Suri's scowl deepened, but she stepped aside so Addy and Shawn could come in. She closed the door and crossed the room.

"Who's he?" Suri asked, falling onto a lime-green couch in the small living/dining space.

Addy sat at the opposite end of the couch

while Shawn leaned a shoulder against the wall separating the kitchen from the living area and crossed his arms over his chest.

"He's a private investigator helping me locate Cassie."

Suri's eyes roamed over Shawn like a predator sizing up its prey.

Addy's dislike for the young woman deepened.

"We know you lied about Cassie leaving town, and we can prove it," Addy said. Maybe not the subtlest approach, but she was low on patience.

"I didn't lie," Suri spat.

"Then why did we find Cassie's clothes and other things in the attic of the apartment you two shared? Cassie wouldn't have moved without taking her things."

Suri squared her shoulders, but Addy read the fear in her eyes before they darted away. "Maybe. I don't know anything about that."

"So someone broke into your apartment and packed up all Cassie's things without you knowing a thing about it?" Addy struggled to keep her voice even against her rising fury.

Suri shifted, pushing her back against the arm of the sofa and putting as much room as possible between them. Still, her voice rang with defiance. "Cassie did talk about moving back to New York."

The *but* hung heavy in the air.

Addy glared silently.

Suri sighed. "The last couple of days before she left or whatever, Cassie was worried or something. She didn't tell me what it was about, but I think she was mad at Ben, or maybe they broke up or something, because she wouldn't take his calls and I know they hadn't been out on a date in a while."

"Why didn't you tell the sheriff about this?" Shawn asked.

Suri shot a look at him, then moved her gaze to the window. One shoulder went up. "I forgot."

Addy leaned forward across the sofa into Suri's personal space. "That's not going to fly."

Suri pushed to her feet and crossed to the television. Snatching a pack of cigarettes and a lighter from the stand, she lit up, blowing a ring of smoke up to the ceiling. "Look, I didn't want no trouble then, and I don't want any now." She jabbed the cigarette in Addy's direction.

Addy stood. "Then tell us the truth."

Suri rolled her eyes. "Fine. Whatever. That guy Teddy came by like two weeks ago and told me to say Cassie had moved back to New York. If you ever meet Teddy, you'll know why

I did what I was told. That guy is deranged." A shudder rocked Suri's bare shoulders.

A picture of Teddy's menacing dark eyes popped into Addy's head.

"Okay, what about Cassie's clothes being in the attic?"

"I don't know anything about that. For real," Suri said when Addy shot a disbelieving look at her across the room. "Teddy said Cassie had left town and her stuff was gone. That's all I know."

"That's not all." Shawn spoke again.

Suri took another drag on her cigarette, blowing it in Shawn's direction.

He didn't blink. "How'd you get your new job and this fancy apartment, Suri?"

"That's none of your business." Suri ground her cigarette out on the side of the TV stand, not for the first time from the marks on it.

"It is if you had a hand in killing Cassie Williams," Shawn shot back.

Everything in Addy revolted at the idea, but she kept quiet and let Shawn press Suri. She recognized the question needed to be asked, and she wasn't able to do it.

Suri's eyes went to slits. "I didn't kill anyone."

Addy swallowed hard, pushing her words past the lump in her throat. "Why lie, then?

Cassie was gone. If you were really afraid of Teddy, why not tell the police what you know?"

"'Cause I have to look out for myself. I'm not a rich girl slumming it before I go off to MIT. When Ben came around offering me a real job and this apartment, I knew it was in exchange for keeping my mouth shut." Suri shrugged. "I didn't see a better offer coming my way, so I took it."

It was obvious Suri was jealous of Cassie. But what kind of person lied about another's disappearance? Her sister could be hurt or worse, and Suri didn't care at all. Her casual disregard for Cassie's safety sent anger pulsing in Addy's veins.

Addy hopped up off the couch, crossed the room and got in Suri's face before Suri processed the action.

"Without a thought for Cassie?" she hissed. "Don't you care at all that Cassie could be in serious trouble?"

Rage nearly blinded Addy. Her hands balled into fists at her side.

"Hey, I said I didn't have anything to do with Cassie disappearing or getting killed or anything like that. For all I knew she did move back to New York."

"Where is Cassie?" Addy yelled, grabbing

Suri by the shoulders and shaking the slighter woman. "What did you do to my sister?"

"Get off me." Suri struggled, trying to push her away, but fueled by a combination of pure fury and fear, Addy's grip on the woman was strong.

Shawn crossed the small space in two steps, dropping a heavy hand on Addy's shoulder. "Let her go, sweetheart. She doesn't know anything more that can help us."

Addy let her hands drop from Suri's shoulders.

Shawn wrapped his arms around Addy's shoulders, and she leaned into him.

"I'm calling the cops," Suri screamed, backing away to the other side of the room. "She assaulted me in my own home."

Somehow she doubted Suri would follow through on the threat, though. Although she would be within her rights to file charges. For the first time in as long as Addy could remember, she had completely lost control.

Shawn gave voice to Addy's thoughts. "Do that. I'm sure they'd be interested in what we have to say about why we came to see you, Miss Bedingfield."

Suri's whole body shook, whether with anger or fear, Addy wasn't sure. Maybe a bit of both. "Get out."

Shawn shot Suri a hard look. "Come on, Addy. Let's go."

Shawn grabbed her arm, but Addy dug her heels into the floor.

Addy locked eyes with Suri. "If my sister is hurt, Teddy will look like a teddy bear compared to what I'll do to you."

Chapter Twelve

Addy had hoped to make it back to the hotel before Shawn. A little time for her nerves to settle before the inevitable argument would have been nice, but the Yukon rode the Mustang's bumper the entire way back to Bentham.

Shawn moved to her side the moment she got out of her car.

"What were you thinking, going to see Suri without me?" A couple passing by them in the parking lot glanced their way, the pace of their steps increasing as they did.

"Don't you think we should have this conversation in private?"

Addy turned and headed for the hotel without waiting for his response. Shawn fell into step beside her, and they rode the elevator in silence. With each passing floor, her anger grew.

Who was he to be angry at her for going to see Suri? Yes, he was helping her, but she was a grown woman. She didn't need his permission to go anywhere.

Not to mention he and his brother seemed to think she might have something to do with Cassie's disappearance in some bid to inherit Cassie's portion of their father's insurance. A thought broke through her fury. Maybe Shawn coming to her aid when he did, injecting himself into the search for Cassie, wasn't a coincidence at all. Maybe he wouldn't tell her about his case because she was his case, and he was investigating whether she had something to do with Cassie's disappearance. But who would have hired him?

The insurance company, maybe, but the small amount of insurance her father had held would hardly warrant an investigation. The money hadn't even covered a third of his medical bills. And the company had already paid out. No, that made no sense.

Still, she couldn't shake the feeling that Shawn's offer to help find Cassie wasn't one hundred percent altruistic.

Shawn opened the door to the suite and let Addy pass into the room.

She rounded on him before the hotel room door clicked shut. "I don't know who you think you are, but I don't take orders from you."

He tossed the key card on the table and met

her head-on. "I didn't order you to do anything. We agreed we'd go see Suri together in the morning."

"We didn't agree to anything," she shot back, pointing a finger at him. "You said you had something else to do. Fine. I didn't. The only thing I care about is finding Cassie, and I'll do whatever I have to do to do that, with or without you."

"You could have been in real danger confronting Suri alone. The lies we already know she's told could put her in jail for a significant amount of time. If it turns out she knows more than she's saying or had a hand in Cassie's disappearance, that gives her even more incentive to keep you quiet."

Addy threw her hands in the air. "I can take care of myself."

"I didn't say you couldn't, but it's stupid to run headfirst into a potentially dangerous situation without backup when you don't have to."

"Backup? Are you referring to yourself? Because I'm starting to question if I do, in fact, have backup?"

Shawn's expression hardened. "What the hell does that mean?"

"Tell me about the case that brought you to Bentham." She fisted her hands on her hips.

"I told you I can't. The client wants to keep it confidential."

"I saw the background check you had West do on me."

Wrinkles appeared on Shawn's forehead. "The background—Addy, we do background checks on all our clients. It's standard operating procedure."

"Except I'm not a client. You showed up at my hotel room with this serendipitous offer to help me find my sister. Why? Why do you even care if you have another case you're working on?"

She watched his jaw clench. "I explained that. I needed a cover that explained why I was in town, and I knew West could help you find Cassie."

"Is that the only reason?" Addy kept her eyes trained on Shawn's face, looking for any hint of deception.

"Addy, why don't you just ask the question you want to ask?"

"I saw your and Ryan's comments about my father's insurance payout. You think I had something to do with Cassie's disappearance. Is that why you're helping me?" The words spilled out of her mouth. "To keep tabs? Prove I hurt my sister for money? Well, if that's your plan, you're going to be disappointed. I would never hurt Cassie. I have no idea where she is, but I don't need someone who doesn't trust me to help me find her."

Addy turned on her heels and stalked into the bedroom. She took her suitcase from the closet and tossed it on the bed before moving to the dresser.

Shawn stopped in the bedroom door, watching her throw her clothes onto the bed.

"For the record, I never thought you had anything to do with Cassie's disappearance." The heat she'd heard in his voice moments ago was gone.

His words were like a pin to the balloon of anger she'd been sailing on. She dropped down on the bed next to her suitcase. "I saw your comment. Motive, question mark." She drew a question mark symbol in the air with her finger.

He sat next to her. "Money is always a motive."

"One man's change is another man's treasure?" She smiled weakly.

"Something like that," Shawn said, returning her smile. "But even if I found a note written in your handwriting saying, 'make Cassie disappear,' I wouldn't believe you'd hurt your sister."

Addy's lips cocked up, and she sent a sideways glance at him. "Now I have to wonder how good a PI you are."

Shawn chuckled. "Okay, maybe in that circumstance I'd start to wonder."

Addy dropped her head into her hands. She wanted to trust him, but she felt fried, unsure whether to trust her instincts. She wasn't even sure her sister was still alive. Wasn't sure she'd ever know what happened to her. She was in no state to judge whether what she felt for Shawn was real or whether he was using her to some end he wouldn't tell her about.

"The case you can't tell me about, is it about me or Cassie? Is somebody, the insurance company or some long-lost relative I don't know about, paying you to find out if I had something to do with Cassie's disappearance?" Her heart squeezed as the words crossed her lips.

She couldn't be sure, but she thought she saw something pass over his face. Whatever it was, it passed too quickly to name.

Shawn pushed the suitcase out of the way and took her hands in his, looking into her eyes.

"Addy, I promise you. I know you love your sister and had nothing to do with her disappearance. I am not investigating you."

The sincerity in his eyes caused her heart to stutter. She'd refused to get close to anyone after her divorce, throwing herself into her job so she wouldn't ever be hurt the way her ex-husband had hurt her again. And what did she have to show for it? No husband and, now, no job. But here was Shawn, still standing by her side, helping her to find Cassie even after she'd pushed him away. Somehow he'd worked his way past her defenses.

She eased closer, raised her hand to cup his chin and kissed him.

He kissed her back, tugging her closer. The sweep of his tongue sent electric shocks through her. After a heated minute, he pulled back.

"We should stop. I don't want you to do anything you regret."

Her entire body screamed that she wouldn't regret being with him. Even after their weekend together, when she'd vowed not to let it happen again, she'd never regretted being with him. She wasn't sure that was possible.

His rejection stung. She scooted back on the bed, putting more distance between them. "You're right. I'm sorry."

Shawn reached out and cupped her cheek. "You have nothing to be sorry for." He rose from the bed and headed toward the bedroom door before turning back. "Sleep tight, princess."

He shot one last look across the room before shutting the door behind him.

Chapter Thirteen

Shawn spent the next several hours reading the background reports Ryan had sent on Suri and Ben and left a message asking for a tour of Spectrum's chip factory.

He also pulled a background report on Lance Raupp. From the superior attitude to the way he'd looked at Addy, the man had seriously rubbed him the wrong way. Ben had the necessary access to pull off the fraud, but Shawn wasn't convinced he had the smarts to pull it off. Lance, with a bachelor's degree in business and a minor in computer engineering, hit all the right notes.

No matter how hard he tried, Shawn's mind kept going back to Addy.

She'd been clear about why she didn't want to get involved. He didn't want to be like her ex, putting her in a position where she felt like she had to choose. He wouldn't do that to her. She'd regretted their first night together, and he couldn't, wouldn't, let her make that mistake again.

He laughed softly, mirthlessly. This was the first time he couldn't get a woman out of his head. He was honest with the women he saw, promising nothing beyond dinner, maybe dancing and a night of fun and pleasure. Some he saw for more than a night, but never much more. Never long enough for any ideas of longevity, much less permanency, to set in.

But look at him now.

One night with Addy six months ago and… and he hadn't been with a woman since.

He'd teased Ryan in the early days of his romance with his now-wife, Nadia, mostly because that's what brothers did. But a part of him had also seen the kind of love Ryan felt for Nadia—the all-consuming need to be with another person, to make that person happy— and he'd wanted it for himself. He wanted it with Addy.

His phone rang, mercifully pulling him out of his thoughts.

It was after midnight. He didn't need to look at the screen to know who called.

"Got the chip," Ryan whispered.

"Why are you whispering?"

"Nadia is asleep." Ryan's wife had just entered her third trimester, and Ryan could barely stand to leave her side. "Analyzing it now. Should have something for you by morning."

"Okay. Thanks."

"What's wrong?"

Ryan could read him better than anyone. Add in that there was only an eighteen-month age difference between them, and it was almost as if they were twins.

It also made it nearly impossible to keep anything secret from Ryan.

"Nothing. I just… Addy. Nothing." Shawn's frustrated sigh was so loud he looked to the closed bedroom door to make sure Addy hadn't woken.

No sound came from the other side.

"Blue balls." Ryan laughed.

"Good night, Ry."

Ryan hung up.

Shawn put on his pajamas and brushed his teeth.

He skipped pulling the sofa out into a full bed and instead grabbed a blanket and two pillows from the closet near the door and stretched out on the couch. He'd slept in much worse accommodations, and he didn't want to take the chance that moving the furniture would wake Addy.

He'd almost fallen asleep when the bedroom

door opened with a click. Shawn sat up on the couch.

"Everything okay?"

Long, silky brown legs showed from under a pale green sleep shirt.

His groin pushed against the front of his pajama pants. He could only hope the darkness of the room hid his desire.

"Yes, I…" Addy took several steps toward the sofa.

Shawn got to his feet, meeting her in the middle of the room.

He curled a hand around her arm. "Addy, what is it?"

She reached up and stroked Shawn's cheek lightly. "That weekend together wasn't a mistake."

His breath knotted in his chest. Whatever he'd expected her to say, it wasn't that.

"It was a rare time I felt free to just be. No job. No responsibilities. I could just be me."

Addy curled her arms around his neck, going to her toes and feathering kisses along his jawbone and down his throat. "And you saw me."

A groan tore from his throat. "Addy."

His resolve was evaporating fast.

She pulled back far enough to lay her hand over his lips. "I know what I'm doing, and I know what I want. I want to not feel scared. I don't want to think. I want to just feel. I want to feel pleasure. I want to feel you. Make love to me, Shawn."

Her lips, soft and sweet, took his in a hard kiss filled with intent and desire.

He slid his hands to her hips and carried her into the bedroom.

No other woman had stirred in him the feelings Addy did. He wanted her, not just physically, but he wanted to be with her. To sit beside her. To talk to her and hold her hand. To laugh with her and fight with her. And not just while they were here in Bentham. For the first time in his life, he wanted to build something real— with Addy.

He just hoped she felt the same way.

Chapter Fourteen

Addy awoke to the sun peeking around the curtains in the room and the bed next to her empty.

The last time they'd slept together, she'd been the one to slink away in the dark of night. Now she knew what it felt like to wake up the next morning alone. Of course, Shawn probably preferred it that way.

It left Addy with a sense of loss and more doubts than she knew what to do with. Not about what they'd done, but about where they'd go from here. Last night had been incredible. After they'd rested a bit, he'd awoken her with kisses down her spine and they'd gone at it again, this time in the voracious way of lovers long kept apart. He'd driven her to heights she'd only read about in the campy bodice rippers she'd sneaked out of the library as a teen. She cared for Shawn more than she should, far more than was prudent.

Trepidation spread through her.

Beyond the personal, she wasn't sure what their night together meant with regard to him helping her find Cassie. Would he decide it was best if they didn't spend any more time together, afraid that she might get too attached?

Too late.

No. Whatever they'd shared, she wouldn't let it stop her from finding Cassie, and she had to admit she needed Shawn's help. Even if things were awkward, she was an adult, and she could handle it.

And if he wanted to return to her bed tonight?

The sounds of the door to the suite opening and Shawn moving around in the other room interrupted her musing.

She tossed the covers to the other side of the bed and crossed to the bathroom.

Sometime in the night, she'd donned her nightshirt again, but that didn't stop her from wrapping herself in the white terry-cloth robe that hung on the back of the bathroom door. She ran a brush through her hair and brushed her teeth and stepped into the common area of the suite.

"Good morning." Shawn flashed what could only be called a satisfied smile.

Her entire body flushed, and she tore her

gaze from his, padding over to the table where he'd set two large paper coffee cups.

She reached for the cup on the left. "Good morning."

He took the cup from her hand before she took a sip, replacing it with the second cup. "You still want to track down Ben this morning?"

Addy took a long sip of coffee, letting the blessed nectar fully awaken her brain. "Uh-huh. Absolutely."

"Okay, then. The coffee is from the continental breakfast downstairs, but I figured we could get breakfast at the diner we ate at yesterday. I need more sustenance than a bagel after the workout you gave me last night."

The unexpected comment had her choking on her coffee.

He patted her back until she caught her breath, a sexy smile on his stubble-roughened face. "I…yes. Breakfast is good. I'm going to grab a quick shower. Maybe we can stop by the sheriff's office, too. We need to make sure Sheriff Donovan knows Suri lied about Cassie leaving town and that Ben and that creep Teddy are somehow involved in all this."

"I left a message for the sheriff last night. We'll follow up after speaking with Ben."

Addy returned to the bedroom and quickly

showered and changed into jeans and a black-and-white-striped top. While she got ready for the day, she tried not to think about last night, which only led to her reliving every amazing moment—and there were many over the several hours Shawn had spent in her bed.

Heat curled in her belly.

She was not looking for a relationship, Addy reminded herself. Last night was magnificent and she wouldn't mind a repeat performance, but she was in Bentham to find Cassie. That's what she needed to focus on.

Her stomach fluttered as she reentered the living room area of the suite.

Shawn looked up from the laptop he tapped away on. "You ready?"

Her stomach growled in answer.

At just after seven in the morning, Bentham's rush hour wasn't quite in full swing yet. The diner was nearly full, but Becky seated them immediately in a booth in the back next to a window facing the surface parking lot where Shawn had once again parked the Yukon.

They ordered, and their food was delivered to the table quickly.

She dived into her pancakes and bacon, eating until the pains in her stomach subsided. Shawn had ordered pancakes and bacon, too, but unlike her golden flapjacks, his pancakes were a muddy brown and surrounded by stringy pink wisps of meat.

She frowned at his plate. "What kind of pancakes are those?"

He grinned. "Whole wheat. And Becky even rustled up some turkey bacon."

She shook her head. "That's just sad."

He laughed at the same time a black BMW swung into the parking lot outside the window.

Ben emerged from the car in a long camel-colored wool coat. As he closed the door, a black motorcycle pulled to a stop behind the car, blocking Ben from leaving.

The motorcycle rider straddled the bike and flicked his visor up. Teddy Arbury.

"Look." Addy pointed to the scene beyond the window.

Ben crossed his arms over his chest, a sour look on his face.

"I wonder what they're arguing about?" Shawn said, setting down his fork.

"With those two, it could be anything," Becky said, slipping up to the table to drop off their check and refill their coffee cups.

Shawn glanced over at Becky. "Why do you say that?"

"Teddy and Ben. They've been friends since high school. Bad seeds, both of them." Her face twisted in a grimace.

Based on her last encounter with Teddy, Addy could understand why Becky didn't care for Teddy. But Ben? Addy knew why she didn't like him. He didn't seem to care at all that Cassie was missing, which was suspicious as far as Addy was concerned. But Becky was referring to something else.

"Ben's a bad seed? He's an executive at a thriving computer company."

Becky tipped her head down to glare at Addy. "Executives can be bad seeds, too."

"Yes, of course," Addy answered, feeling chastised.

Becky shot her one more glare before continuing, "They went to high school together. An odd pair on the surface, but underneath they're more alike than not. Both selfish and entitled. Ben's money always got him out of the consequences, and I think that's why Teddy hitched his wagon to Ben's horse. You know where one goes, so goes the other."

The three of them watched as Teddy stabbed the air between him and Ben with a finger before roaring off on his bike. Ben walked out of view of the window, and Becky moved to refill the coffee cups of the couple at the next table.

"I'd love to know what that was all about," Shawn said, shifting to get his wallet from his back pocket.

Ben walked in and strode to the counter as Shawn spoke.

"I'm more interested in the tension Suri mentioned between him and Cassie," Addy answered, scooting off the bench. "Either way, let's not waste the opportunity to ask him."

Shawn followed as she wove between the booths and tables to Ben's side.

A young red-haired waitress handed Ben a paper cup, smiling coquettishly. Ben winked and turned away, stepping back in surprise when he saw Addy standing in his path to the door.

"Oh, Addy. How nice to see you again," Ben said in a politely distant voice.

"We finally tracked down Suri Bedingfield. She was under the impression you and Cassie argued right before Cassie went missing."

Ben smoothed the blue tie around his neck. "I can't begin to fathom why she'd think that. Cassie and I were no longer together, but we parted on good terms, as I told you."

Ben's expression remained placid, but he swallowed hard.

She cocked her head to the side and put on a faux-pleasant tone. "Yet Suri seems to think otherwise. Why is that?"

"You'd have to ask her," Ben said with a plastic smile.

Addy could feel the tether she had on her temper fraying fast. She moved closer to Ben's table, crowding into his personal space. "We also found Cassie's things thrown into garbage bags and stuffed into the attic at her apartment. You know anything about that?"

"I can't say I do," Ben said, his voice hard.

Addy bent forward, putting her face within inches of Ben's. "I know you're lying. I know you had something to do with my sister's disappearance." She slammed her hand down on the table. "Where is my sister?"

It took everything in her not to hit Ben. To pound on him until he told her where to find Cassie.

Shawn grabbed her arm and inched her away from the table.

Ben took the opportunity to slide out of the booth. "Look. I've told you what I know." He glared at Addy. "I don't like being harassed."

"I'm sure you can understand how upset Addy is," Shawn said in a conciliatory voice.

Ben's gaze slid to Shawn. "I need to get to work."

"Pretty early to be going into the office." Shawn cut Ben off as he attempted to move around Addy to the door.

"Yes, well, I need to head out to the factory before going into the office."

"Hey, why don't we go with you?" Shawn said, cuffing Ben's shoulder. "You did promise a tour."

Ben frowned. "I don't know."

"Then we won't be in anyone's way," Shawn said with an unnaturally bright smile.

Ben's frown deepened, but then he nodded. "Let me just make sure it won't be a problem."

Ben moved several steps away and pulled out his phone.

Addy's eyes narrowed on Shawn's face. "Why are you so interested in the Spectrum factory? It has something to do with the case you came to Bentham to investigate, doesn't it?"

Addy watched as Shawn's gaze moved from Ben to her. "You know I can't tell you about that. I can drop you off at the hotel."

"I'm going with you."

Shawn's brow furrowed. "I don't know if that's a good idea."

Addy's stomach twisted. Shawn was still keeping something from her, and she'd never fully trust him until she knew what it was.

"I don't care." He started to argue, but she cut him off. "Look, we can kill two birds with one stone here. I know you have confidentiality issues with this other case, but I hope by now you know you can trust me."

"I do trust you."

That simple declaration made her happier than she had time to examine at the moment. "Good. So there's no reason I can't go. Cassie was there at least two days a week. Someone may know something that could help us find her." Addy cut her eyes toward Ben. "And I want to talk to him some more. I think he knows more than he's saying about where Cassie could be."

She caught Shawn's glower out of the side of her eye but ignored it.

"You want to follow me?" Ben said, returning.

"Sure," Shawn said without enthusiasm.

A zing of electricity shot through Addy when Shawn put his hand on the small of her back as they followed Ben out of the diner.

Ben got in his BMW, and Shawn followed him from the parking lot.

"You really think Ben isn't connected to Addy's disappearance?"

Shawn followed the BMW onto a two-lane county road leading south. "I don't know. I just don't think we should jump to conclusions. Especially not based on evidence from Suri Bedingfield."

"Her sudden move to Garwin is suspicious, as is that fancy apartment."

Shawn's gaze moved to the rearview mirror.

"Exactly. And she had just as much opportunity, if not more, to hide Cassie's things in that attic."

She released a heavy sigh. "I just want to find Cassie."

He reached for her hand without taking his eyes off the road and squeezed. "I know, and we will."

He moved his hand back to the steering wheel, his eyes flicking to the mirror again and his jaw tightening.

"Why do you keep looking in the mirror with that worried expression?" She turned in her seat to see what he was looking at. There was very little traffic on this road, only Ben's BMW in front of them, a motorcycle coming up fast behind them. "Is that Teddy? What's going on?"

"Make sure your seat belt is on," Shawn answered.

She watched as the motorcycle advanced on the Yukon.

The motorcycle followed dangerously close. What was this idiot doing? He would rear-end them if he didn't slow down. "Shawn?"

Addy's adrenaline spiked. She faced forward in time to see Ben's BMW speed up on the street in front of them.

Shawn pressed the accelerator, switching lanes to avoid a slow-moving white-paneled van.

The motorcycle switched lanes behind them, speeding up to keep pace. The road ahead of them was clear, but a drag race down the highway was still dangerous.

Addy reached into her purse for her phone.

The motorcycle put on a burst of speed and pulled up next to them on Shawn's side of the car.

Addy tried to look past Shawn at the person driving the motorcycle, but she could only catch a glimpse of the face of a white male with a dark beard before Shawn hit the gas, throwing her back against the seat.

A succession of pops sounded at the same time Shawn yelled, "Get down!"

She froze, struggling to make sense of the sounds she'd heard and where they were coming from to heed Shawn's warning.

The popping sounds came again, and this time her brain processed exactly what they were. Bullets.

Addy shrank down in her seat so her head dipped below the passenger side window. She still held her phone in her hand. She quickly dialed 911, relating where she and Shawn were and that they were being shot at.

Shawn veered wildly to the right and onto the shoulder of the road. On either side of this section of the highway, there was nothing other than miles and miles of land.

Shawn got them back onto the pavement and put on another burst of speed in an attempt to outrun the bike. The motorcyclist kept pace behind them, but close enough that a sporadic volley of shots pinged off the back bumper. A bullet smashed through the back windshield, and a scream tore from Addy's throat.

Shawn ducked down, sending the Yukon swerving wildly. "Are you okay?"

She slid farther in her seat, nearly sitting on the floorboard. "Yes. But he's trying to kill us!"

"It certainly seems so."

Shawn swore, his gaze locked on something ahead of them.

She pushed upward enough to see through the front window.

A sharp curve with a steep drop-off loomed up ahead. The roadside sign cautioning drivers to slow down whizzed by, followed closely by another deeming the speed limit thirty-five miles per hour.

They were moving at well over twice that suggestion, and the continued shots coming from behind them cautioned against slowing.

Shawn gripped the steering wheel tight

enough to turn his knuckles white. He tapped the brakes as they rode into the turn at a still much too fast speed.

The gunshots had stopped, but there was little time to give thanks.

The cyclist drew even with them again and swerved to the right. Metal screamed as the passenger side of the Yukon scraped along the barrier.

"Hang on!" Shawn stomped on the gas, sending them shooting forward again.

They were still in the curve, but a straight stretch of highway loomed in front of them.

The motorcycle slammed into the back of their car, sending them spinning.

Shawn struggled to regain control of the Yukon as it sailed across the center line. Luckily, there was no oncoming traffic.

They slid from the road, the driver's side of the car scraping along the barrier until they made it to the end.

But the Yukon didn't stop. It careened backward through the tall grass along the side of the highway, miraculously halting just before they would have plowed into a line of trees.

"Are you all right?" Shawn's voice sounded like it was coming from underwater.

Addy looked at him. A large gash slashed his temple, sending blood dripping down the side of his face. The sight sent a wave of fear through her, almost as strong as the one she'd felt when she realized Cassie was missing. But he was conscious and talking, so that was good.

"I'm okay, I think." She wiggled her fingers and toes and mentally scanned herself for injuries. A sharp pain radiated from her side, but it didn't feel too bad. She was dazed, but like Shawn, she hadn't lost consciousness and counted that as a win.

"I can't get out. My seat belt is stuck, and the door is jammed." Shawn pulled on the seat belt, but it didn't give.

She tried her seat belt, unsnapping it easily. Somehow the airbags hadn't inflated, which was a godsend, because if they had, they wouldn't have been able to see that they weren't out of the woods yet.

They'd stopped some twenty yards from the road near the end of the curve in the highway. From their vantage point, she could see a green pickup idling at the side of the road up ahead.

Fear and adrenaline rushed through her. She bent forward, scanning the floorboard beneath her feet, running her hand under the passenger chair, looking for her purse. It wasn't there, which meant her Ruger inside it wasn't there, either. The force of the crash could have easily sent it sliding to the rear of the car or even out of the now-missing passenger window.

"Where's your gun?" Addy asked without taking her eyes off the truck.

Shawn followed her gaze to the truck.

"In the glove compartment."

Addy prayed the glove box would open and breathed a sigh of relief when it did.

A black-and-silver pistol lay in the glove compartment next to a full magazine.

She grabbed the gun, inserting the magazine and checking that the safety was off.

"What are you doing?" he asked, attempting to reach for the gun but wincing.

"Preparing to defend us if it becomes necessary."

The bike lurched forward, swinging into a U-turn as she spoke. The truck began slowly moving in their direction on the wrong side of the road.

Where the hell were the police? It seemed like it had been hours since she'd called 911, although her rational mind told her it had been only a minute. That had been all it had taken to be shot at and driven off the road. She knew in her gut the police wouldn't make it in time to save them.

"Lean your chair back," Addy said, crawling over the console separating them. There was no need to let down the window. There was no window anymore.

"It's too dangerous. Let me do it." Shawn attempted to reach for the gun in her hand. The fact that she could easily swat his hand away told her everything she needed to know about which of them should hold the gun.

Addy scrambled over his legs. "We don't have time to argue about this."

Addy positioned herself so she had a clear shot at the cyclist.

The motorcycle crawled closer. The rider's arm rose, a gun in his hand.

The driver was male, but Addy still couldn't get a good look at his face.

She stopped trying and focused on the gun.

Her grandfather's voice rang in her ears.

It's all muscle memory, baby doll.

Sweat beaded on her forehead.

The driver raised his gun. She drew in a deep breath, then let it out as she pulled the trigger.

The driver's scream echoed over the empty highway. His gun fell onto the asphalt.

Addy kept the gun trained on the truck as its tires squealed. The rider turned toward her, the absolute hatred on his face sending a chill down Addy's spine. She recognized Teddy.

The motorcycle sped away.

"He's gone," Addy said, crawling back into the passenger seat. "It was Teddy Arbury."

Shawn swore.

She could hear the sounds of sirens in the distance.

"Sounds like help is on the way," Shawn said, peering through the windshield.

"Good." Addy handed the gun to Shawn. She didn't think Teddy would come back, but the calculation as to who was better off defending them if he did was rapidly changing. She reached under her shirt, touching her abdomen. She came away with her fingers covered in blood. "I think I need it."

Chapter Fifteen

Shawn paced the hospital waiting room.

The EMTs had whisked Addy away while the fire department cut him out of his seat belt. He'd waived treatment and had a deputy drive him to the hospital. He'd been so desperate to assure himself that Addy was okay that he'd forgotten to lie and say he was her fiancé or husband when the nurse had asked. Now no one would tell him anything about Addy's condition because he wasn't immediate family. He was nearly out of his mind with worry.

Shawn turned to head back the length of the room and spotted Donovan.

"This is quite a mess you and your lady friend got yourselves into," Donovan said.

"Not one of our making," Shawn growled.

"So you told my deputy. I retrieved Ms. Williams's purse from the vehicle. Thought you might want to hang on to it for her." Donovan handed Addy's purse over. "I'm afraid your vehicle is going to be a loss."

Shawn glanced inside the purse, checking to make sure her gun was properly secured in the purse holster.

One of Donovan's eyebrows cocked higher than the other.

"She has a New York permit to carry," Shawn said.

Donovan lifted his chin. "I know. If she didn't, she'd be headed straight for my jail from her hospital bed. How is she?"

He ran a hand over his head. "I don't know. No one will tell me anything because I'm not related. But there was a lot of blood. I think she might have been shot."

Donovan took pity on him. "Hang on. I'll see what I can find out," he said, exiting the waiting area and striding toward the nurses' desk.

Shawn was monumentally pissed off at himself. He'd messed up big-time, putting the only woman he'd ever cared about in danger. Nearly getting her killed.

Bile rose in his throat at the memory of seeing her covered in blood. That Teddy had been the one to fire the shots absolved him of nothing. It was his fault for putting her in the situation in the first place. He should have known better.

Shawn had given Ben an opening, and he'd taken it, setting them up to be shot. Had someone at Spectrum found out why Shawn was really in town? Or were the bullets meant to stop Addy from looking for Cassie? Maybe both?

If Addy hadn't been such a crack shot, they both would have been killed.

Another memory of Addy slumped next to him in the passenger seat of the Yukon, her hands covered in her blood, flashed through his mind.

It had been close. Too close.

Footsteps fell in the hall, the sound growing louder as they did. Someone was headed his way. He looked up, expecting to see Donovan, and was surprised to see Ryan and Gideon instead.

He'd called Ryan soon after arriving at the hospital, but unless they'd learned how to appear by magic, there was no way Ryan and Gideon should be standing in front of him right now.

"What are you doing here? How are you here?" Shawn asked, rising and meeting the other two men in the middle of the room.

People had always commented on how similar the West brothers looked. A half inch shorter than Shawn, Ryan was stockier and preferred to keep his face and head cleanly shaven. But compared to Gideon, he and Ryan were downright diminutive.

Six foot six and roughly the width of a sedan, Gideon had muscles with muscles. He'd served in the military with Shawn's oldest brother, James. Even West's contacts and investigative powers hadn't successfully turned out a full background check on Gideon. No doubt the missing periods in Gideon's life would stay that way until the United States government wanted it otherwise. But James had vouched for his friend and fellow soldier, and that had been more than enough. Gideon had quickly proved himself an asset to the firm.

"We were on our way when you called. How is Addy?" Ryan dropped a heavy hand on Shawn's shoulder.

Gideon, the quintessential man of few words, only nodded.

"I don't know. No one has told me anything." Shawn expelled a breath. "Why were you on your way to Bentham?"

"We got the report back on the chip you found in Ben Konstam's office. It's a fake."

"I'm not surprised. I'm sure Konstam is also behind Addy and me being shot at," Shawn replied.

He'd given Ryan a quick and dirty summary of the shooting in their call, but now he elaborated on the chance meeting with Ben at the diner and that he and Addy had been following Ben to the factory when they were shot at.

"I want to know where Konstam and Arbury are now," Shawn said, aiming a look at Gideon.

Gideon nodded briskly, moving to the other side of the waiting room and pulling out his cell phone. Gideon had cultivated an extensive network of contacts and snitches that had come in handy on more than one West investigation. If anyone could get a bead on Konstam and Arbury, it was Gideon.

"The fake chip alone isn't enough to prove the bad chips weren't manufactured by Intellus," Ryan said. "Intellus wants us to get enough evidence to show the authorities and the public that they aren't responsible. We need to show that Spectrum is making these chips and falsely using the Intellus logo to undermine their brand."

That was easier said than done. The only way to definitively show that Spectrum was behind the fraud was to get into the factory. Since they only had a couple of days, if that, to get the proof they needed, an undercover operation was out of the question. That meant they'd have to get into the factory and document the fraud without being discovered. They'd pulled off similar operations before, but the tight time frame made doing so riskier than Shawn would have liked.

Before he could voice his concerns, Donovan strode back into the room. His step faltered for just a moment at the sight of the three men before he recovered. It wasn't the first time the three of them together had had that effect on others.

Shawn stepped around Ryan and spoke to Donovan. "Did they tell you anything?"

"She wasn't shot. A piece of glass from the broken window lodged in her side. They got it out and are stitching her up now."

Relief flooded through him like ice-cold water on a hundred-degree day.

"Who are your friends?" Donovan asked, his gaze homed in on Ryan.

Shawn introduced Ryan and Gideon to Donovan. The men shook hands, and Donovan turned back to Shawn. "Why don't you tell me what happened out there?"

Shawn recounted the call from Ben this morning and being ambushed on the drive to Spectrum's factory.

Donovan shot him a skeptical look when he got to the part where Addy shot the motorcycle driver.

"She shot the gun out of his hand?"

Shawn couldn't keep a proud smile from

spreading across his face. "Technically, I think she shot him in the forearm, but yes, she shot him and he dropped the gun."

"While the motorcycle was moving?" The question came from Ryan, who seemed just as skeptical as Donovan.

Gideon, who'd rejoined the group of men while Shawn recited the chain of events, maintained a poker face. If Gideon was surprised or doubtful, he never showed it.

Shawn's smile grew wider. "It was a damn sight to behold, but it saved our lives. Teddy Arbury tried to kill us."

Donovan scratched something in his notebook. "How can you be sure it was Teddy?"

Shawn explained seeing Teddy on his motorcycle outside the diner not long before the attack. "It looked like the same bike."

Donovan frowned. "But you're not sure? You didn't see the face of the shooter?"

"No." Shawn scowled. "I didn't. But Addy did."

Donovan scratched a note on his pad. "And how do you know Edward Arbury?"

"I don't. The first time I met him, Addy and I were at the diner and Teddy cornered her coming out of the ladies' room. He made a veiled threat about backing off investigating Cassie's disappearance, and I stepped in. It didn't go any further than that, mostly because the waitress put Teddy in his place, and Addy and I left right after."

"And you have no idea why Teddy would have approached Ms. Williams?"

"I didn't then. Did you get my message about the chat Addy and I had with Suri Bedingfield?"

This time Donovan frowned. "I got it. Want to explain what you were doing in Garwin?"

Shawn checked his temper and walked Donovan through his and Addy's questioning of Suri, leaving out his mad dash to get to Addy and her assault of Suri.

"So Miss Bedingfield just admitted to you two that she lied?" Donovan's eyebrows rose until they nearly touched his hairline.

"We asked some very pointed questions. Ms. Bedingfield correctly deemed it to be in her best interest to answer truthfully. I might be more skeptical of Suri's story if Ben Konstam hadn't just set us up."

Donovan narrowed his eyes. "What do you mean, set you up?"

"We were following Ben from the diner to the factory."

"So Edward Arbury and Ben Konstam are working together to get Ms. Williams to give up the search for her sister. Why?"

Shawn felt, rather than saw, Ryan tense beside him. He knew how Ryan felt about keeping the client's confidence, but it was time to bring Donovan in on his real reason for being in town.

Shawn explained Intellus's discovery of fraudulent chips marked with their logo and how they'd hired West to root out the source.

Donovan's lips puckered with irritation. "You should have told me what you were up to—"

Ryan interrupted before Donovan could continue his dressing-down. "You have your obligations, and we have ours."

The two men stared at each other with twin scowls.

"Ben made a call before we left the diner. I'd bet good money if you pull his phone records you'll find that call was to Arbury."

They didn't have time for posturing or hurt egos. It was becoming increasingly clear to Shawn that Ben Konstam was the key to whatever was going on.

"Your suspicion isn't enough to pull Konstam's phone records," Donovan said dismissively.

Shawn felt a vein along the side of his neck throb in annoyance. "Did your office get an emergency call from Ben about the shooting? He had to have seen us getting shot at."

Donovan's brow furrowed. "No. The only call we got was from you."

First Cassie disappeared and now he and Addy were shot at. Not to mention the attempted mugging the night Addy got to town. He was convinced the events were related. He hadn't gotten a good look at the attacker's face, but his size and weight were similar to Teddy's. The situation had escalated, and they still had no concrete idea why. It seemed unlikely that the chip fraud he was investigating and Cassie's disappearance weren't connected somehow. But if Cassie was a participant in the fraud, why had she disappeared? The obvious answer was one none of them wanted to think about, but with every passing day, it became harder and harder to overlook.

"I think Ben and Teddy had something to do with Cassie Williams's disappearance and the fraud and are trying to hide it now."

Donovan exhaled loudly. "Yeah, it's looking more and more like that."

Some of the tension that had built up inside him evaporated. At least Donovan was considering the possibility.

"Addy's convinced Cassie is alive."

Donovan shook his head. "I'm sure you know how hard it is for family members to accept these things. Especially if there isn't a body."

"I know, but Addy is a reasonable person. If she believes Cassie could still be alive, we'll keep looking."

Out of the side of his eye, he saw Ryan frown.

Donovan ran a hand through his hair. "I can't stop you, as you well know, but whatever is going on here is dangerous. Think about that." Donovan directed a pointed look at Shawn. "In the meantime, I've put an all-points bulletin out on Teddy Arbury, and I've got a deputy on the way to Garwin to see if Suri Bedingfield will come in to give a statement."

"What about Ben Konstam?"

"I'll talk to him," Donovan clipped out.

A balding man in round-rimmed glasses and a hip-length white lab coat entered the waiting room. The stitching on his coat read Dr. E. Jackson.

His eyes scanned over the four men in the room. "Shawn West?"

"That's me." Shawn approached the doctor, his heart rate picking up speed.

The nurses had been adamant about not being able to tell him anything about Addy's condition. If the doctor was looking for him now, did that mean that the worst had happened?

"If you'll come with me, you can see Ms. Williams."

Shawn paused long enough to get the keys to the car Ryan and Gideon had driven to town and the approximate location of where they'd parked. Ryan and Gideon planned to pick up a rental and head back to the hotel.

Shawn followed Dr. Jackson down a long, bright white hallway with signs directing them at various intervals to the ER, ICU and cardiac areas of the hospital.

"I thought I wasn't allowed to see Addy," Shawn said, lengthening his stride to keep pace with the doctor. Though he was about six inches shorter and thirty years older than Shawn, Dr. Jackson moved swiftly down the hospital hallway.

Dr. Jackson rolled his eyes. "Strictly speaking, you're not. But Ms. Williams has been demanding to see you since she got here. I just finished her stitches, and I'm concerned she's going to pop them trying to get out of bed and get to you, so…" He threw up his hands, stopping in front of a blue-curtained area. "I'm working on her discharge papers now. I'll be back with them in a moment."

Shawn pulled the curtain back.

His breath caught in his chest when he saw Addy lying on her back, her face ashen. She'd pulled up the green scrub top she wore and was examining the bandage on the left side of her stomach.

She glanced up at him and smiled. "Hi."

"How are you feeling?" He came to a stop at the side of the bed.

She pulled the hem of her shirt down. "Like I got stabbed in the side with a piece of glass."

"Don't joke." He smiled weakly for her sake, but he couldn't remember ever being more afraid than he'd been when the EMTs had driven her away from the scene of the shooting. He kissed her forehead, then, as softly as he could, her lips.

She grabbed his hand when he moved to pull away and squeezed. "You were trapped in the car. I was worried, too. How's your arm?"

He raised his arm over his head and rolled his shoulder. "A little sore, but nothing a few industrial-strength aspirin couldn't handle. That was some shooting."

Addy's right eyebrow rose higher than the left. "I told you I grew up on a ranch. I know how to shoot."

"West has employees who are ex-military who couldn't have made that shot."

Addy shot him a lopsided grin. "I'll host a class for them when we get back to New York."

She glanced around him at the large circular desk, where two nurses and Dr. Jackson stood.

An electric menorah decorated one end, and a small Christmas tree stood on the other.

"Did he tell you when he's going to let me out of here?" Addy jerked her head in the doctor's direction.

"He's working on the discharge papers now."

"Good." Addy swung her legs over the side of the bed. "Ooh. Ah," she grimaced, grabbing her side.

"Take it easy." Shawn put his arm around her and helped her up from the bed.

He tamped down the rage that swelled at Addy's pain. Teddy better hope Donovan found him before he did.

Dr. Jackson returned with Addy's discharge papers, a prescription for painkillers and instructions to have her primary care physician look at the stitches in a week.

"Has the sheriff picked up Teddy yet?" Addy asked as they exited the hospital.

"Donovan is looking for him."

"Good. Teddy must have followed us from the diner."

The hospital's visitor lot wasn't large or anywhere near full, so he spotted the dark blue SUV easily. Shawn opened the passenger door for Addy. "The question is how he knew when we would leave the diner."

He watched realization spread across Addy's face. "Ben set us up."

"It looks that way."

Addy edged into the SUV slowly.

Shawn gritted his teeth, watching her breathe through the pain.

"Suri would have told them we talked to her. We need to find Ben now. If he and Teddy are desperate enough to try to kill us, there's no telling…" Addy's voice trailed off.

He stepped into the space between the car and the open door. "I know you believe Cassie is alive, but, sweetheart, it may already be too late."

Addy put her hand on his arm. "I'm not in denial. I can't explain it. I know she's alive, and I have to keep looking until I find her."

Her expression was equal parts earnestness, determination and fear.

The knowledge that she could be wrong, that it could already be too late for Cassie and to avoid Addy's heart breaking, made his chest tighten. He wanted desperately to protect her from the possible pain, but he knew he couldn't.

Shawn leaned forward and placed a soft kiss on her lips before backing up and closing the door.

As he drove them to the hotel, he thought about the fact that Addy would never be able to move on without knowing what happened to Cassie, one way or the other. And if that's the closure she needed, he'd make sure she got it.

Chapter Sixteen

Shawn exited the pharmacy with the painkillers Dr. Jackson had prescribed for Addy, a bottle of water and plastic wrap.

He could see Addy through the car's windshield as he approached the SUV. Her head rested against the seat, and her eyes were closed.

He felt a slap of anger. He'd get Addy settled in the suite, and then he planned to find Ben Konstam.

His phone beeped as he got into the car. A text from Jorge, the Spectrum employee he'd spoken to at the bar the night before.

We need a guy to help load the trucks. 6pm. You in?

It was after three, which didn't leave him, Ryan and Gideon much time to figure out strategy, but this was their best chance for getting the evidence Intellus needed to prove their innocence.

Shawn sent back a single word. In.

Jorge texted Shawn an address he recognized as the Spectrum factory.

"Something important?"

He looked up from the phone and into Addy's eyes.

Even banged up, she was the most beautiful thing he'd ever seen.

"A possible break in the other case I'm working on." He popped the top on the pain pill bottle, handed her one and then opened the bottled water and gave that to her as well.

She swallowed the pill and half the bottle of water before speaking again. "I know I've taken up most of your time, and I haven't said thank you. Thank you."

He swept a lock of hair from her cheek, tucking it behind her ear. "Finding Cassie is my priority, I promise you."

His heart raced when she leaned her cheek into his palm.

"I doubt your brother feels the same way," she said, looking at him from beneath long lashes.

"Let me handle Ryan."

She pressed a kiss to his palm. He leaned forward, dipped his head and caught her mouth in a sweet, gentle kiss. He could have sat there forever kissing Addy, but his phone rang.

"You on your way back?" Ryan spoke without preamble.

Shawn put the car in gear, backing out of the parking space. "Yeah. I had to stop by the pharmacy first, but we're about ten minutes out. Got a text from a guy who may be able to help on our case."

He glanced across the car at Addy, but her eyes were closed. He still hadn't told her about his suspicion that Cassie might be involved with the ring producing fraudulent computer chips.

With each passing moment, keeping that information from Addy felt increasingly wrong.

"We can talk about it when I get back," Shawn said, ending the call.

He navigated the streets of Bentham back to the hotel. Addy hadn't stirred. He hated to wake her, but carrying her was out of the question. Not only because he was sure the gesture would mortify her, but his shoulder, while nowhere near as bad as her injury was, still throbbed. He'd bought a bottle of extra-strength Tylenol when he'd picked up Addy's prescription and planned to take one as soon as he got to the suite.

Hopefully, the pain medication would keep most of the pain at bay, because he'd be loading who knows how many trucks come six this afternoon.

"Addy. Addy, sweetheart, wake up. We're at the hotel."

She woke slowly, which he assumed was partly a result of the pain medication she'd taken. The pharmacist had warned that it could leave her drowsy.

He gave a moment's notion to calling Ryan or Gideon and asking them to carry Addy in, but banished the thought almost immediately. No way was he going to let another man carry his woman.

His woman.

He'd never once thought of a woman as his before. He'd been a part of protection details on more people, more women, than he could remember, and with each one he'd felt a duty to protect that went beyond collecting his paycheck. This was different, though. As cavemannish as the idea was, the need to protect Addy specifically was primal—and more than a little disconcerting, because he knew that if anything ever happened to Addy, he'd be lost.

He shook himself out of his introspection and helped Addy from the car and up to the suite. He helped her remove her shoes and get into bed. She was asleep before her head hit the pillow.

He snapped the bedroom door closed and took out his phone.

"We're back," he said when Ryan answered.

Ryan hung up without a response, and less than five minutes later, a knock sounded on the door.

"We've got to keep our voices down. Addy's asleep," Shawn said, letting Ryan and Gideon into the room.

"She okay?" Gideon asked, taking a seat at the table.

"Yeah. The glass cut deep but missed everything vital," Shawn answered.

Ryan crossed to the couch in the room and sat. "Good. Now, what's this about a text?"

Shawn caught Ryan and Gideon up on his strides in Intellus's case: his trip to the bar last night, the conversation with Jorge and his subsequent text offering Shawn a job loading Spectrum trucks this evening.

"That doesn't leave us a lot of time to prepare," Ryan said, waking the tablet he'd brought into the room with him.

"No, it doesn't, and since I don't want to leave Addy alone, it means there'll only be two of us," Shawn countered.

Ryan frowned without looking up from the tablet. "We don't have a lot of time to get the evidence we need for Intellus. If Addy stays in the room, she should be fine by herself."

Gideon leaned back in his chair, folding arms the size of tree trunks across his chest. A rare smile breaking out across his face. "I hear she's a hell of a shot."

Ryan laughed, but Shawn didn't join in.

"She's on painkillers. Teddy targeted us this morning, and we have no idea where he is. I checked with the hospital while I waited on word about Addy, and no one with a gunshot wound to the arm checked in."

Ryan's serious expression had returned. "Donovan would have alerted hospital staff to notify him if Teddy came in. He won't show up there."

"Probably not, but we can't be sure he won't come here trying to finish the job. It wouldn't be hard to figure out what hotel we're in, and we don't know if Teddy is onto me for looking into the fraud or if he wants to keep Addy from searching any further for Cassie," Shawn said.

"Could be both." Ryan stroked his chin. "We still don't know that Cassie Williams isn't involved in the fraud, but it's safe to assume Ben and his buddy Teddy are knee-deep in it. Could be that they want to stop your investigation and Addy's."

Shawn shook his head. "I don't know Cassie,

but she and Addy seem close. I can't believe she'd allow Teddy to hurt her sister."

Ryan shot Shawn a dark look. "It wouldn't be the first time one family member turned against another. Especially when money is in the mix."

Shawn had seen enough close friends and family members turn on each other to know the truth of Ryan's statement. His gut told him that Cassie wasn't involved in the fraud. Still, that didn't mean she wasn't aware of it—knowledge that could put her life in danger.

"Gideon can stay with Addy. You can handle surveillance and serve as backup." Shawn sat on the couch next to Ryan.

Gideon nodded his acceptance. Ryan's only answer was a frown.

Annoyance rumbled through Shawn. He and Ryan needed to have a long talk when they'd closed the Intellus case. Ryan might be president of West Security, but Shawn was as much an owner as he was. It was past time for Ryan to start acting like it.

For now, Shawn focused his attention on the tablet. He described the exterior layout of Spectrum's factory and where would be a good spot for Ryan to hide with the video camera. Shawn would be wearing a body camera and mic that would catch the Spectrum employees if they discussed the fraud. It was also his responsibility to get a shot of the chips that were being shipped. That would be hard if the boxes were already sealed, but he'd manage.

Ryan's job was to get the long shot of the dock while the boxes were being loaded and document which trucks the boxes went into. Hopefully, between them, they'd get the evidence they needed to prove Spectrum was behind the fraudulent Intellus chips tonight.

Then he could focus solely on finding Cassie.

They refined their plans and strategy until five, when Ryan left for the factory to get set up without anyone seeing him. They were lucky the days were shorter. Ryan was a master of hiding in plain sight, but the cover of darkness would come in handy. It was probably also why Jorge and his crew were starting the loading so early instead of later in the evening. If the employees cleared out in streams at five thirty like they had the day before, the factory would be deserted by six.

At five minutes to six, Shawn pulled into the small parking lot at the back of the factory near the loading docks. Jorge, Granger and two other white men waited on the docks.

Shawn put on square-framed glasses that hid a camera and mic and climbed out of his car to meet the men where they stood.

"Glad you could make it, amigo," Jorge said, extending a hand.

Granger shot a suspicious look at Shawn and ambled away to the other side of the loading dock while Jorge introduced the other men, Harris and Leon, the assistant manager.

Once he and Leon settled on a price for his labor, Shawn and the other men got started loading the three trucks.

By the end of the first hour, his arm ached, but he'd been able to peek into several boxes, finding nothing except computer chips marked with the Spectrum logo. A second hour passed, and he finished loading the boxes without finding any evidence of fraudulent chips.

Shawn pocketed the cash Leon handed him and drove back to the hotel.

Ryan parked beside him and slammed out of the Expedition. "Please tell me you got something?" He crossed his arms over his chest.

Shawn's irritation spiked upward at Ryan's attitude. "Nothing." He handed Ryan his glasses. "The chips I saw looked legit. They were all marked with Spectrum's logo."

Ryan's nostrils flared. "Damn it, Shawn. We're running out of time here," he snapped.

Shawn felt his jaw clench. He mimicked Ryan's stance by folding his arms over his chest. "We both know how these things go. Sometimes you spend hours on a stakeout or days working a contact and get nothing. It's not the first time."

Ryan stepped closer. "Intellus is sure the next shipment of fraudulent chips is going to hit the market in the next day or two, and they won't be able to keep it out of the press this time."

"I know that. I'm doing everything I can," Shawn ground out. He'd been putting off broaching the idea of telling Addy the whole truth, but if they weren't able to find evidence that Spectrum was behind the fraud, it would come out, regardless. He didn't want Addy to find out that way. "Look, Cassie is tangled up in all this somehow, maybe as an innocent, maybe as a player in the fraud. Either way, I think it's time to tell Addy everything."

Ryan shook his head. "We promised Intellus we'd keep this quiet."

"And we are. I trust Addy. She's not going to run to the press."

"You've known her for, what, a day? Two days? Come on, Shawn." Ryan snorted.

Shawn stepped into his brother's personal space. "Why don't you just say what you mean? It's not Addy you don't trust. It's me."

"Don't put words in my mouth," Ryan snarled.

"I don't have to. You've been second-guessing, checking up and generally riding my ass like I'm some rookie from the get-go. When's the last time you questioned how Gideon executed on one of his cases?"

"Gideon doesn't get distracted. You're more worried about saving a girl who might not need saving so you can impress her sister than you are about our client."

Shawn's hands balled into fists. Growing up in a household full of testosterone-led males, physical fights weren't unheard-of. It had been a long time since he'd punched one of his brothers, but at the moment, he itched to clock Ryan. Maturity held him back.

Instead, he stepped in closer to Ryan so they were only inches apart.

"Then I guess I'm more like you than either of us realized," Shawn said.

Nadia, Ryan's wife, had been a client of West Security when they'd gotten together.

Ryan glared.

For a moment Shawn again thought they might come to blows, then Ryan let out a deep sigh. "We don't have time to argue. We still need proof Spectrum is behind the fraud."

Shawn took a step back, a tacit agreement to a truce. "Then I suggest we go up and plan out our next steps. If my instincts are correct, the girl you think might not need saving and the fraudulent chips are connected. And if we're running out of time, so is she."

Chapter Seventeen

Shawn and Ryan found Addy and Gideon finishing dinner when they returned to the suite. The first thing Shawn noted was that sleep seemed to have done a world of good for Addy. The ashen pallor that dusted her face in the hospital was gone, and she attacked the Thai noodles on her plate with her usual vigor.

She turned a brilliant smile on him, sending a punch of desire through him.

"We got enough for both of you," she said, pointing to the takeout containers in the center of the table.

He smiled wanly and dropped into the chair next to her, reaching for the food. "Thanks."

Addy shot him a questioning look, but he focused on the curry chicken in front of him.

Ryan picked up the last takeout container. "I'm going to bring this back to my room."

"I'll head out, too," Gideon said, rising and tossing his empty container in the garbage.

Moments later, Ryan and Gideon were gone.

Addy tilted her head, looking at him. "It couldn't have been anything I said."

"It's not you. Ryan's pissed at me. Don't worry about it." He speared a piece of chicken and chewed.

"I guess whatever you two were up to tonight didn't go well."

He shook his head. Finding Addy awake meant he, Ryan and Gideon weren't able to talk about the Intellus case. He was sure Ryan would take care of bringing Gideon up to speed, but they'd have to wait until they could be alone to plan their next steps.

Not that he knew what the next steps should be.

He was confident Ben was at least aware of the fraud. The chip he'd found in Ben's desk seemed evidence enough of that. But was he in on it? And how did the fraud connect to Cassie's disappearance?

Addy seemed content to let him eat and ruminate. His phone ringing broke the silence in the suite.

"Shawn West."

"I didn't have anything to do with you getting shot at." Ben's shrill, almost frantic voice rang out.

Shawn put the call on speaker, motioning for Addy to stay quiet as he did.

"I have a really hard time believing that, Ben," Shawn replied, his voice hard.

"I didn't, I swear. I mean, Mr. Raupp saw that note you left for me asking for a tour of the factory. I called to ask him if it was okay to take you on a tour of the factory, but I didn't know he'd send Teddy after you."

Lance Raupp. It made sense. Ben was in the perfect position to orchestrate the fraud, but he lacked the mental firepower to pull it off. Not like Lance, who was smart enough to organize the scam and offer up Ben as the fall guy.

Of course, Ben's declaration of complete innocence rang hollow. Ben had taken that two-lane county highway on purpose, leading them right to Teddy. But arguing with him wasn't going to get Shawn what he wanted, so he put it aside for now.

"This whole thing is out of control," Ben screeched into the phone. "I just wanted to make some extra cash."

"What's out of control? Why would Raupp send Teddy Arbury to shoot at us?"

"Oh, man. This is really bad. Teddy, that guy isn't all there."

"Ben?" Shawn was quickly losing patience with the conversation.

"Look, all I did was package and deliver some fake computer chips. No big deal, but then Cassie figured out what was going on and Raupp said she needed to be dealt with."

A strangled squeak came from Addy's throat. Shawn squeezed her hand and lifted a finger to his lips, indicating she should remain quiet. He didn't want Ben realizing she was listening in and clamming up.

His instincts had been spot-on. Cassie was mixed up in the fraud, but she'd discovered it— she hadn't been a part of it.

"How did you deal with her?" Shawn asked.

"Me? I didn't do anything but help Suri get a job out of town. Teddy is the one who dealt with Cassie."

Tremors shook Addy's body.

Shawn prayed the answer to his next question wouldn't break her. "Is Cassie still alive?"

"I… I'm not sure. I think so," Ben stammered.

Addy's breath released in an audible whoosh.

"I overheard Raupp and Teddy talking about keeping her alive until the next shipment of chips goes out. Look, I need your help. I know you're some big-shot PI from New York City. The last shipment goes out tonight. Once those chips are delivered, Raupp won't want to keep either of us alive."

Could Ben be playing them again? Shawn hadn't been able to look inside every box he'd loaded earlier that evening, but none of the ones he'd opened had contained fraudulent chips. Their best bet was to get their hands on Ben and get the whole story as soon as possible.

"Where are you?" Shawn asked.

"I'm… I'm at my grandmother's old place—it's been empty for years. I figured it was a good place to hide under the radar for a while, but Raupp is bound to look here eventually. I need to get out of town."

"What's the address?" Shawn grabbed the hotel notepad from the television stand. He jotted down the address while Addy keyed it into her phone's GPS.

"You have to come get me," Ben demanded.

Addy turned her phone screen outward so Shawn could see it. The GPS put the address about twenty minutes away from the hotel.

"Sit tight," he said ending the call and immediately making another.

"What's wrong?" Ryan asked when the call connected.

Shawn filled his brother in on the call from Ben. Before he'd finished, a knock sounded on the suite door.

"Could be another trap," Ryan said, striding into the suite.

Gideon followed with a large black duffel bag that Shawn knew held a number of devices useful for various excursions.

"That's why I need you and Gideon to go with me."

Ryan set the laptop he carried on the table and went to work. Shawn knew he was pulling up maps of the area as well as real estate info and whatever other information he could find on the address Ben had given them.

"Ben said Cassie was still alive," Addy added. She'd been silent since Ben's call. Shawn hadn't pushed, allowing her space.

Shawn took her hand in his. "Ben has a lot of reasons to lie right now."

"I've got to hang on to hope."

The last thing he wanted to do was to take away her last fragment of hope. If this was another ploy by Ben to attack them, they'd cross that bridge when they got to it.

"Let's go, then," Addy said, looking from Gideon to Ryan before her gaze landed on Shawn.

Shawn shook his head. "You're staying here."

"No way. I've come this far, and I will see this to the end."

"I put you in danger once already today." He put a hand on each of her shoulders, turning her toward him. "It's not going to happen again."

Addy gripped his wrist. "Shawn, I am a grown woman. I understand there are risks, and I'm willing to take them."

He shook his head.

"If you leave me, I'll just drive myself."

His mind worked overtime to come up with a way to keep her at the hotel. Given Teddy's determination this morning, Shawn wasn't comfortable leaving Addy at the hotel alone, anyway. He wasn't taking any chances this time. He needed Ryan and Gideon for backup when he approached Ben. Taking Addy with them would keep her close, and if she waited in the car while they secured Ben, she should be safe.

"You'll go with us, but you have to do what we say. It's the only way we can be sure you'll be safe."

Addy's mouth turned down, but she nodded.

Ryan's gaze moved from the computer screen to Shawn. "Gideon and I picked up a rental after we left the hospital. We can follow you two to the house."

Minutes later they were in their respective vehicles and rolling toward Ben's grandmother's house. A light snow fell as they drove, reflecting off the car's bright headlights.

Ben's grandmother's neighborhood was older, built when homeowners expected more than an arm's-length worth of land between their home and their neighbor's. The houses that lined the street in a neat row of symmetrical brick squares were worn and time battered, the occupants more concerned with survival than home repair. Here and there, multicolored lights had been strewn around a tree or an inflatable Santa waved from a front yard.

Shawn parked the SUV behind Ryan's rental three houses down from the address Ben had given him.

Ryan and Gideon met Shawn and Addy in the darkness between the two cars.

Ryan glanced from Addy to Shawn. "How do you want to play this?"

"I'll go through the front." Shawn looked at Ryan and Gideon. "You two come through the back."

Ryan nodded and opened his hand. Three small earpieces sat in his palm. Shawn and Gideon each took one.

"What about me?" Addy asked.

"You stay in the car," Shawn said, fitting the earpiece in his right ear.

"I already told you—" Addy began.

"And now I'm telling you. You stay in the car until we clear the house. I'll come get you when we know it's safe." When she looked like she was ready to argue, he softened his tone and added, "Addy, please."

She scowled. "Okay. But I want to be there when you talk to Ben."

"Done," he promised, relieved that she'd agreed without further argument. No matter what, he was determined that she would not be hurt again.

Addy returned to the car, and he waited until he heard the door locks click into place before motioning for Ryan and Gideon to take up stations around the house.

The exterior of Ben's grandmother's home was covered in chipped, faded white stucco. Rotten wood fencing encircled the overgrown front yard.

Shawn walked along the crumbling concrete walkway, his eyes scanning back and forth for shapes lurking in the adjacent yards or too-curious faces in neighboring windows.

An American flag rippled on the house next door, but unsurprisingly he saw no one. It wasn't a neighborhood where it paid to be curious.

He waited for Ryan and Gideon to round the side of the house before climbing the front steps to the porch.

Just in case someone was watching, Shawn

kept his gun in its holster under his jacket. He knocked on the front door. "Ben? It's Shawn West."

Nothing but silence answered from inside.

He attempted to peer through the window at the side of the door, but it was covered with years of grime, making it impossible to see anything inside.

Shawn knocked again, then tried the door. It opened easily.

"Front door is unlocked," he said, knowing Ryan and Gideon would hear through their earpieces. "Going in."

Shawn stepped inside, pulling his gun.

The cold temperatures had done nothing to quell the smell of garbage and animal feces that permeated the air. Only abject fear and desperation would lead a person to seek shelter in the house.

"Front room clear," Shawn said.

"Coming in the back door." Ryan's voice came through Shawn's earpiece.

"Ben? Are you here?" Shawn called out again.

He inched past the faded burgundy velvet couch in the den and the aged yellow linoleum flooring in the kitchen. Almost everything in the house was covered in a thick layer of dust, but the kitchen table had been wiped clean, and a single plate and cup were in the sink.

In his line of work, Shawn had learned to trust his instincts, and he had a bad feeling about the current situation. It smacked of a setup, but if there was even a small chance that Ben knew where to find Cassie, it was a chance they had to take.

"Basement's clear." Ryan's voice came through the earpiece.

"Kitchen clear. Holding here," Gideon responded.

The home's two bedrooms were at the back of the house.

"Ben? It's Shawn West," he called, identifying himself again in case Ben was afraid to come out of hiding.

The house was still.

He and Ryan converged at the opening to the hallway leading to the bedrooms and a single bath in the house.

Ryan motioned, signaling he'd clear the first room.

Shawn nodded and moved to the second door on the right.

A heavy wooden dresser lined one wall and a woman's dressing table sat against the other. A four-poster bed stood between them. A single pillow and a tousled blanket lay across the otherwise unmade bed.

Ben lay on the floor at the foot of the bed. Shawn swept the closet quickly to make sure no one hid in the room.

It looked like Ben had been wrong about no one looking for him at his grandmother's, but he'd been right to be scared. It had taken less than thirty minutes for Shawn and Ryan to get to Ben's grandmother's house, but they'd still been too late.

Shawn crouched next to Ben. The bullet hole in Ben's head left no doubt that he was dead, although the still-congealing blood indicated he hadn't been that way for long.

"The house is clear." Ryan's voice came in stereo through the earpiece and from behind Shawn.

Shawn stood and moved aside, giving a clear line of sight from the door to Ben's body.

Whatever Ben knew about Cassie or the fraudulent chips, he'd never reveal now. Ben's killer had gotten to him quickly. And by all appearances, they had just missed Ben's murderer.

How had the killer known where to find Ben and that he'd been about to tell all?

Shawn scanned the small room for Ben's cell phone but didn't spot it. The killer might have taken it with him in an effort to conceal his communication with Ben. They'd probably never know. If Ben's killer had his phone, he'd certainly destroy it the first chance he got.

Shawn and Ryan backed from the room. They made it back to the living room as Addy came through the front door.

Shawn swore. He stepped in front of Addy, putting his hands on her shoulders to keep her from barreling down the hallway they'd just come from.

"Where is he? Did he tell you where Cassie is?" Addy craned her neck to see around Shawn.

He looked down at her. "You can't go back there, Addy."

Addy's expression was fierce. "Move, Shawn." She tried to shake his hands off, but he held firm.

"Listen to me. Ben's not talking to anyone. Addy, he's dead."

She froze.

"No. He…he can't be. He knows where Cassie is. He knows."

He pulled her to him, holding her as her shoulders began to shake with sobs. "I'm sorry, sweetheart. I'm so sorry."

Chapter Eighteen

Shawn shot Addy another concerned look. The last of several since they'd left the police station. He mercifully hadn't tried to engage her in conversation. She didn't have it in her to talk anymore right now.

Sheriff Donovan had been apoplectic when he'd arrived at the scene. He'd threatened to arrest all four of them and probably would have if he could have found any cause. At the station, the sheriff had asked a hundred questions a dozen different ways, even after she'd told them she hadn't seen anything. After hours of questioning, he'd finally let them go well after midnight.

Addy felt hollowed out, yet she wanted to scream.

They were so close. Deputies had found Cassie's scooter in a shed in the backyard, but no sign that Cassie had been at the home.

She was sure Ben had known more than he'd told them, maybe even where Cassie was being held.

"I'm not going to find Cassie. She's probably... I'm probably too late."

"Don't say that." Shawn reached a hand across the middle console, but Addy pressed into the side door. "We're doing everything we can, and we'll keep doing everything we can."

"I'm always too late." She'd been too late in noticing her ex-husband pulling away. Too late seeing how sick her father had become. And now, too late to save Cassie. The words looped around her heart.

The SUV jerked as Shawn slammed into a parking space in the hotel's parking lot.

He turned to her and took her by the shoulders. "Stop! You're doing the best you can."

"That's just it. My best is never good enough! No matter what I do, the people I care about just keep leaving me, no matter what I do."

Shawn wrapped his arms around her. She clung to him, shaking with silent sobs. She couldn't remember ever crying as much as she had in the last several days. But for a few precious minutes, she put down the mantle of the strong sister and daughter and let herself fall apart. It probably meant something that she felt comfortable doing so with Shawn, but she'd have to save that analysis for a time when she wasn't having a nervous breakdown.

After several minutes, she gathered herself. They walked from the car to their room, Shawn's arm around Addy's shoulder, hers around his waist. As much strength as she drew from Shawn's presence, what she really wanted and needed was time to sift through her emotions alone.

Addy crossed to the bedroom, turning back to look at Shawn before going in. "I'm going to take a shower." She needed a nice long soak in the suite's Jacuzzi tub, but she'd have to wait until she got her stitches out. The injury to her side throbbed, and she desperately needed a painkiller.

In the bedroom, she grabbed the pill bottle from the bedside table and swallowed two pills with a glass of water from the bathroom sink. Her torso muscles still felt like a tight rubber band on the verge of snapping. Until that night it had been easy imagining Cassie was still alive. But Ben's murder moved the entire situation into a new, much more dangerous place.

She started the shower, then padded into the bedroom while the water warmed to grab a change of clothes from her suitcase. She could hear Shawn's and Ryan's voices, low but still audible through the closed door. They weren't arguing, exactly, but the tone of the conversation was tense. She pressed her ear to the bedroom door, catching more of the conversation.

"I honestly don't know. I'm sure Ben is involved in both the fraud and Cassie's disappearance, but there's no hard evidence the two things have anything to do with each other," Shawn said.

"Cassie Williams knows computers, and she worked at Spectrum. She could be in on the fraud, too," Ryan responded.

His words reminded her that Ben had mentioned something about delivering fraudulent chips when he'd called. That must be the other case Shawn was in town for. But what did Cassie have to do with any fraud?

Addy swung the door open and marched into the living room.

Ryan sat on the sofa, Shawn across from him in an armchair.

"Are you insane?" Addy fisted her hands at her sides, glancing from Shawn to Ryan. "Cassie would never have gotten involved in any fraud."

She noted that the utter surprise on their faces would have been comical in another situation. But at that moment, she was too angry to laugh at anything. She turned to Shawn. "Is this the case you've been working on? Have you been investigating Cassie?"

Shawn rose from his seat. "I'm not investigating Cassie." He glanced at his brother before training his gaze back on Addy. "I'm investigating the production of fraudulent computer chips. We think Ben is somehow involved."

"And Cassie?" Addy took a step backward, putting space between them. She felt like the pieces of a puzzle had just snapped into place in her mind, and she finally saw the whole picture. "That's what this has been all along. You helping me but really trying to find Cassie because you think she's involved in your other case."

"That's not true." Shawn moved toward her.

She shot both hands out in front of her, stopping his progress.

"I considered whether Cassie could be involved in the fraud, but I never believed it. Addy, you have to believe me." Shawn's gaze beseeched her.

He sounded sincere, and her heart cried out for her to believe him.

"We have to consider the possibilities," Ryan said from his perch on the couch. "Whether you want to believe it or not, your sister has the knowledge to do something like this. The disappearance could be her way out." Ryan crossed his arms over his chest.

Addy shook her head. "You have no idea what you're talking about."

Shawn cut off the rest of her rebuke. "Someone at Spectrum is behind the fraudulent chips—I think it's safe to say that's the case—and they've been manufacturing the frauds for a while, starting well before Cassie began working with the company."

"Maybe they recruited her? It is somewhat strange for a young woman to move from New York City to a relatively small town. Or Spectrum could have just gotten lucky when Cassie walked in looking for a job." Ryan continued to argue his point.

Ryan didn't know her sister like she did. Cassie was kind and gentle. She believed in doing the right thing, even when it was difficult. She never would have taken part in fraud.

"What about what Ben said when he called? Lance Raupp kidnapped Cassie."

"We can't take anything Ben said at face value," Ryan answered.

"You just want to believe the worst of Cassie to give your client a scapegoat."

Ryan didn't respond.

The drum of the still-running water in the bathroom filled the silence. Addy turned back to the bedroom. She shut off the shower in time to hear someone knocking on the suite door.

Hurrying back to the living area, she caught Gideon strolling into the room.

"I just got a tip on Teddy's whereabouts." Gideon stopped in the center of the room, looking at them each in turn. "What's going on?"

"Nothing. Whaddya got?" Ryan answered.

Addy wasn't finished with this conversation by a long shot, but with Ben dead and not enough evidence to pressure Lance into coming clean about his part in whatever was going on, Teddy might be the last hope for finding Cassie alive.

Gideon's expression remained skeptical, but he let the matter drop. "Teddy is holed up at a girlfriend's place the next town over. My source says he has a bullet hole in his arm." He quirked an eyebrow at Addy.

Ryan moved back to the couch and pulled the laptop into his lap.

Gideon, Shawn and Addy followed suit, each one pulling a chair over from the dining table. Gideon relayed the information he'd gotten from his source. Addy had seen the town name on an exit sign on the highway between Bentham and Garwin. As far as Gideon's source knew, Teddy was still there.

Ryan called up a satellite map of the address, and after several minutes of strategizing, the guys settled on a plan of approach.

"Okay, what time are we leaving?" Addy asked, looking from one brother to the other.

Ryan gave a hard shake of his head.

"You can't come with us," Shawn said.

Now Addy stood, too. "Cassie's my sister, and I am not going to sit around while she's out there needing my help."

"This is not a place you want to be," Ryan said.

"It's not safe. Teddy shot at us once already," Shawn agreed.

She wanted to argue with him. She could probably wear him down until he gave in, but to what end? Her side still ached, and all she'd do was slow them down. What she wanted, what she needed, was information that would help her locate Cassie. If hanging back was the best way to get it, then she'd do what she had to do.

"Fine."

Shawn reached for her hand, stopping her before she walked away from the table.

"We will find Cassie."

She prayed with everything in her that he was right.

ADDY FINALLY GOT into the shower after Shawn and Ryan left to track down Teddy. The hot water helped loosen up the muscles in her body. From being shot at to finding Ben dead, cords of tension wound around her muscles. She stood under the shower until the hot water ran tepid, then got out. Try as she might to turn off her thoughts, her mind kept going back to Ryan's ridiculous suggestion that Cassie could be involved in fraud.

Cassie was a sweet, kind computer nerd. She wanted to make technology accessible for everyone, to use it for the common good. She wouldn't be involved in stealing from members of the community she loved being a part of. Cassie had once returned to the grocery store to pay for a bag of chips a cashier had forgotten to ring up. Cassie would have gone straight to the sheriff if she'd known about any fraud.

But what if Addy was wrong? Was the big-sister lens through which she saw Cassie painting a picture of Cassie that was rosier than what the rest of the world saw?

She grabbed clean underwear from her overnight bag and put it on before shimmying into pajama bottoms.

Her cell rang on the bedside table. A local number she didn't recognize.

"Hello."

"Addy?"

The weak but familiar voice sent Addy's heart into her throat.

"Cassie! Cassie, where are you?" Tears of

relief streamed over her cheeks, leaving wet splotches on her shirt.

"Ms. Williams, you and your sister have been far more trouble than either of you are worth, so if you want your sister, come get her." Addy's pulse raced. The cultured voice that flowed through the line was Martin Raupp's.

"Where is she?" Addy stripped off her pajamas and pulled on the jeans she'd worn that day.

"Our old fabrication facility on Route 29. I'm willing to let your sister go, but if you involve the police, well, I'll have nothing to lose then. Understood?"

Addy snatched her purse from the coffee table and headed for the door of the suite.

"How do I know this isn't a trap?" She headed out the door as she spoke.

"You don't."

The line went dead.

Addy ran down the hall, forgoing the elevators for the stairwell. She hit the heavy door with enough force to send it flying open and pounded down the stairs, the phone still in her hand.

She ran across the parking lot to the Mustang, sliding behind the wheel while she dialed Shawn's number. Her heart pounded hard enough that she wouldn't have been surprised if he heard it on the other end of the line.

His phone went straight to voice mail.

She let loose with a string of swears and barreled out of the parking space. "Shawn, Raupp just called me. Cassie is alive. He's holding her at his factory on Route 29. I'm headed there now."

She prayed she wouldn't be too late.

Chapter Nineteen

The ride to Chatham was quiet. Shawn attempted to push his pique aside as Ryan drove. Confronting a man who'd already shot at him once was dangerous enough without negative emotions clouding his judgment. It was hard. Every protective instinct he had had been triggered as Ryan and Addy argued. He wasn't objective when it came to Addy—he couldn't be. He loved her.

"Listen, what I said earlier about you being distracted. I was out of line questioning your work ethic." Ryan broke the silence.

Shawn shook his head. "Now is probably not the best time for this conversation."

Ryan shot him a half smile. "We don't know exactly what we're about to walk into. I don't want you mad at me." As usual, they were on a similar wavelength.

"For real," Ryan continued. "You're an asset to the company, and I don't say that enough."

"Thank you. And look, I know I could step up more on the administrative side of things. You have a new wife and a baby coming. When we get back, I will do better."

Ryan rolled his eyes, but there was humor in them.

"You'll have to show me the ropes, of course, but I'm serious. If I want you to treat me like a co-owner, I need to act like one."

"Okay. Okay. Let's not get ahead of ourselves. I'm still the president of the company, but I appreciate you stepping up. I'm going to want to spend some time with Nadia and the baby after she's born."

"It's going to be so fun to watch you with a daughter one day." Shawn laughed.

As they drove closer to the address Gideon's source had given them, the houses they passed appeared more run-down and the businesses fewer and fewer. They both sobered.

As they neared the location, the tension in the car ratcheted up. Given that Teddy had tried to kill him and Addy this morning, they planned to approach with guns drawn, but the seedy, run-down nature of the surrounding neighborhood only accentuated the potential danger.

Shawn drove slowly past the three-story brick apartment building where Teddy was supposedly lying low. A dirt yard fronted the structure and wound its way around to the back where residents parked their cars. A dirty vertical window traversed the center of the building, revealing an interior stairwell. There were lights on in several of the apartments on either side.

It was a few minutes after 2:00 a.m. They had no idea if Teddy was still inside the apartment, but if he was Shawn was determined to make the man talk.

Shawn pulled into the parking lot behind a neighboring apartment complex, and the three of them got out of the car.

They each checked their guns, then slid on tactical vests. They fit their earpieces and did a sound check before moving toward the building.

It wasn't the first time they'd worked together, and they each knew their role. Shawn approached slowly from the front, keeping to the shadows. Ryan circled, approaching from the back. Gideon hung back, keeping an eye out for anyone coming up behind them.

Ryan came around the building, meeting Shawn at the front door.

"One exterior exit at the rear. Requires a key to enter from the outside," Ryan said.

"I'm on it." Gideon's voice came through the earpiece.

"We're going in the front now," Shawn said, following Ryan through the unlocked front door.

The unit Teddy hid out in was on the second floor. They stopped in front of unit twenty-three, Ryan to the right of the door and Shawn to the left.

Shawn counted to three, mouthing the numbers so he didn't tip off the occupant of the apartment to their arrival.

On three, Ryan kicked the door open, sending it crashing against the wall.

The apartment was a studio with a small kitchenette tucked into a corner.

Teddy lay on a threadbare brown couch barely off the floor. On the floor next to the couch sat an old flip cell phone, a nearly empty bottle of rum and a Glock.

For a moment Teddy stared, wide-eyed like a deer caught in headlights, as Shawn came through the door and advanced toward him. Then he lunged for the gun.

Shawn got there first, kicking the gun under the couch and grabbing Teddy's injured arm.

"Ahhh!" Teddy cradled his arm against his chest.

Ryan cleared the small bathroom and came to a stop next to Shawn. They waited a moment for Teddy's caterwauling to quiet.

Shawn kept his gun trained on Teddy. "Teddy, we have some things we need to discuss."

"I ain't saying shit to you." Teddy pushed himself into a sitting position using his good hand. He'd used a belt and a dirty white T-shirt to make a tourniquet for his arm. His legs splayed open on the couch, his beady green eyes cloudy and unfocused as a result of pain and booze. The grayish pall of his skin suggested he'd lost quite a bit of blood.

"Now, now, Teddy. There's no call for that kind of language," Shawn said.

"You shot me!"

This was interesting. Teddy hadn't noticed it was Addy shooting from their vehicle. They might be able to use that information later, but for now, he was happy to have all Teddy's anger focused on him.

"So we're just going to ignore that you were shooting at us first. That's cool. I'm willing to let bygones be bygones, Teddy. Who shot who is so this morning. What I want to know is where is Cassie Williams?" Shawn said.

"Screw you, man," Teddy spat out. Then his mouth curled up into an ominous smirk. "You're too late, anyway. The delivery is going down now, and Raupp's going to kill the women right after."

Icy shards of fear spread through Shawn. "Women?"

Teddy laughed sinisterly. "Raupp's decided to get rid of both the Williams sisters. That oldest one has really pissed him off, and she's a threat to his operation. He won't tolerate that."

Fury and fear tangled in Shawn's stomach. "Where? Where would Lance hold them?"

Teddy smirked. "You don't have a clue."

Shawn's heart raced in fear, but he held the gun steady and put two bullets in the bottom front panel of the couch between Teddy's legs.

Out of the corner of his eye, he saw Ryan move to cover the apartment door, in case the shots brought curious neighbors. In a neighborhood like this one, it wasn't likely that a couple of muffled shots would lead anyone to call the cops, but they knew better than to take chances. Cops meant questioning, and if Teddy was telling the truth, he didn't have that kind of time.

A string of swears burst from Teddy's mouth. He covered his groin with his good hand. "What the hell? You almost shot off my junk."

"The next shot I won't miss," Shawn said. "Where are they?"

"You won't get there in time, anyway."

"Then it hardly seems worth losing your

manhood over, but it's your call." Shawn raised the gun a fraction of an inch higher. "I won't ask again."

Teddy's eyes widened in fear. "All right, all right. Raupp called your girlfriend about a half hour ago. Told her to meet him at the factory if she wanted to see her sister alive. He told her to come alone, but he's expecting you."

Shawn glanced at Ryan. "We've got to go."

Ryan jerked his head toward Teddy. "What do you want to do with him?"

"We can't wait for Donovan." Shawn pulled a pair of handcuffs from his vest. He hauled Teddy up from the couch and pushed him toward the kitchenette.

"Sit," he ordered Teddy.

Teddy lowered himself to the scarred linoleum with a grimace.

Shawn snapped one side of the handcuff around Teddy's wrist and the other around the handle on the stove. "We can call Donovan to come get him from the car."

Teddy pulled at the stove. "You can't leave me like this."

"Be grateful, Teddy. You were this far from becoming a eunuch," Shawn said, closing the apartment door.

Shawn pulled out his phone and dialed Addy's number as they burst from a side door out into the trash-strewn yard surrounding the apartment building. Gideon met them at the SUV.

Addy didn't pick up, but she'd left a voice mail message. His blood chilled as he listened to the message.

"Martin Raupp. He's got Cassie. Addy's gone to meet him."

Ryan swore and started the SUV. "Martin Raupp? The father?" Ryan swore again. "That's what Teddy meant when he said we don't have a clue. We were looking at the wrong Raupp."

Shawn called out the address Addy had left on the voice mail, and Ryan plugged it into the GPS. "I know this address, but I can't place it." He frowned and dialed Tansy.

Ryan gunned the SUV out of the parking lot.

"Sup?" Tansy answered.

"On my way to an address. It's familiar, but I can't place why." Shawn gave Tansy the address and listened as computer keys clacked on the other end of the line.

Less than a minute later, she spoke. "It's the address for that building Spectrum previously leased. It was in the initial research I gave you on the company. There's a recent real estate listing putting it up for rent, so looks like it isn't in use."

He remembered now. Carrier-Forest LLC. He'd planned to research the property, but so much had happened since he'd rolled into Bentham, investigating a warehouse that Spectrum no longer used had slipped his mind.

He saw now what a mistake that had been. Empty property made for an excellent place to hold someone against their will.

"It's empty, but who owns it?" Shawn asked, although he suspected he already knew the answer to that question.

"Hang on," Tansy replied. A moment passed before she spoke again. "Deed's in the name of Madeline Raupp."

"Damn. I should have caught that," Shawn said after he'd signed off with Tansy.

Martin probably counted on no one thinking about a property Spectrum no longer operated out of.

"We gotta get there now. Raupp has got to be desperate by now. His entire scheme is crashing down around him."

Ryan pushed the SUV to go faster.

Shawn checked the safety on his gun as the neighborhood flew by outside the car's windows. "If Raupp has touched a hair on Addy's head, I'll send him straight to hell."

Chapter Twenty

Addy found the factory easily. A large, faded for-rent sign stood sentry at the entrance to the empty parking lot fronting the drab single-story square building. The weak glow from the one functioning lamppost near the building's door did little to cut through the darkness.

Ignoring the faded white lines marking the asphalt, Addy pulled to a stop directly in front of the spiritless gray building. A large metal loading door was set into the wall of the building next to the glass-fronted main entrance.

Martin stepped out of the glass doors as Addy stopped the car. She reached for her purse in the passenger seat, slinging it across her body.

Martin stepped outside, sticking close to the cover granted by the alcove entrance. Security on either corner of the building sent light bouncing off the silver pistol in Martin's hand. He peered at the car, then scanned the parking lot beyond. "Where's your boyfriend?" Martin's words dripped with disdain.

On his way, I hope, Addy thought. "I came alone." She swallowed the fear clogging her throat. "Where is Cassie?"

Martin scanned the expanse of the building again. "Inside." Martin stepped aside and motioned to the door with the gun. "Now."

Addy passed Martin, ignoring his smirk.

Any furniture in the space had long since been removed, leaving only threadbare gray carpeting and a chipped and scarred reception desk.

"Down the hall to your left." Martin prodded her in the back with the gun.

Addy flinched, her grandfather's voice floating through her head. *It's never the gun's fault. It's always the idiot who's holding it.*

They walked down a long laminate-tiled hall, the click of the heels of Martin's loafers the only sound in the cold, otherwise empty corridor. Despite being in the process of committing any number of felonies, he'd managed to dress the part of genteel businessman in tailored brown slacks and a crisp white button-down.

"In the office on your left," Martin said, motioning to a closed door.

Addy glanced over her shoulder at him. If this was a trap, she could be walking to her death.

But the voice she'd heard on the phone was Cassie's, which meant her sister was alive or at least had been twenty minutes ago. If there was any chance Cassie was inside this room, she had to go in.

Addy reached for the doorknob, turning it slowly. She pushed the door open and froze.

Cassie sat in a desk chair, her left wrist cuffed to a large black filing cabinet. Her hair was a rat's nest of tangles and knots, and her face was slimmer than it had been the last time Addy saw her, but she was alive.

"Cassie!" Addy raced forward, kneeling so she could wrap her sister in a hug.

"Addy, I'm sorry." Tears rolled down Cassie's gaunt cheeks, her shoulders shaking on a sob.

"No, honey. Don't be sorry. None of this is your fault. We're going to get out of here."

The sound of the door snapping closed drew both their attention. Addy's gaze fell on Martin Raupp, whose gun remained trained in their direction.

"I'm sorry, but I think you know I can't let that happen."

Addy straightened and put herself between Martin and Cassie. Cassie peeked around Addy's side, her hand slipping into Addy's. "You said you would let Cassie go."

Martin shrugged. "I lied. I've got to make a very important delivery tonight, and you girls are going with me."

"Why? Why not just leave us here and go? Too many people know you're behind the fake computer chips. Your fraud is over."

"You're so confident you're right," Martin sneered. "From where I'm sitting, the only people who know anything are staring down the barrel of my gun. And both of you are going to disappear. For good this time," Martin said.

A wave of fear crashed through Addy, followed by the determination that she couldn't let Martin Raupp win. Cassie had managed to stay alive for nearly two weeks. Addy just needed one shot at Martin to bring him down.

"At least answer me this," Addy asked to keep Martin talking and buy time. "Why? You're a well-respected businessman. Spectrum is a successful business. Why risk everything you've built?"

"Call it diversification. Spectrum is a little fish in a very big pond. Frankly, there's a great deal of money to be made in cyberfraud. Plus, there's the added bonus of destroying the competition."

"Greed and jealousy," Cassie said.

Martin's face twisted in anger. The hate-filled glare he shot Cassie made Addy's mouth go dry. Cassie's grip on her hand tightened.

"None of that explains why you kidnapped my sister," Addy offered quickly. The last thing she wanted was to make him angry.

"Your sister stuck her nose in where she shouldn't have," Martin spat.

Cassie glared back at Martin. "Ben showed me one of the fake chips. He was drunk and he told me all about the fraud."

"Idiot," Martin snarled. "I should have known better than to bring him in on it, but I needed delivery drivers who had, shall we say, malleable ethics to make the extra deliveries off the books. Then he blackmailed me into giving him a management job." Martin's snarl morphed into a cold smile. "I didn't mind killing him at all."

"I told Ben he should go to the sheriff. That what Martin was doing could get him in a lot of trouble when it came out, but Ben wanted the money." Cassie shook her head forlornly.

Martin scoffed. "Sheriff Donovan. I'd be surprised if Donovan can spell fraud, much less be able to spot one. He's only interested in two things—upholding the illusion that there's no crime in Bentham and getting reelected. Three

guesses who his biggest political donor is."
Martin's smile grew wider.

Cassie wheeled the office chair she sat in so
she was beside Addy. "Ben wouldn't go to the
sheriff, so I decided to go myself. But I wanted
some proof. He caught me going through his
files after work." Cassie jutted her chin in Martin Raupp's direction.

"That dolt Ben had just told me you knew
about the fraud. I was trying to figure out what
to do about it when I saw you going through
the files. I knew you wouldn't be bought off.
I had my little friend here." Martin gestured
with the gun. "And I was able to persuade Miss
Williams to partake in a little staycation in my
basement."

Martin looked pleased with himself.

"And you had Ben and Suri Bedingfield
tell the sheriff Cassie had moved back to New
York." Addy filled in the rest of the blanks.
Cassie's gasp told Addy she hadn't been aware
of that part of the story. "Did you think no one
would come looking when Cassie didn't make
it back home?"

Martin flicked his wrist, looking at his watch
before focusing back on Addy. "Don't you watch
the news? Women traveling alone going missing
is nothing new. Even if a relative came looking,
that had nothing to do with me or Spectrum."

Martin's eyes darkened. "I guess I underestimated you. It won't happen again."

He took several steps to the left, away from the door. "Big sister, you get over there." He waved Addy toward the corner of the room opposite Cassie.

Addy hesitated. Martin was clearly done with talking, but it wasn't clear exactly what he planned next. Attempting anything was risky in the small room, particularly given Cassie's limited mobility.

"Now! And keep your hands where I can see them," Martin growled.

Addy did as he said, moving to the side of the desk. A few sheets of computer paper and a glass paperweight the size of a large marble were the only items on the desktop.

Her heart thundered in her chest as she watched Martin approach Cassie. If he turned just a little more, she might have a chance.

Martin stopped short of turning his back on Addy. He pulled a handcuff key from his pocket and tossed it at Cassie without taking his eyes off Addy. "Uncuff yourself."

Yes! They had a much better chance of overpowering Martin together. Cassie was weak, but Addy knew her sister would fight for her life. Knowing her sister, Cassie was probably more than a little pissed off at Martin Raupp.

Cassie fumbled with the key in her nondominant left hand. Martin kept his gun trained on Addy, but his irritated gazed flicked to Cassie. "Hurry up!"

As discreetly as she could while Martin wasn't looking, Addy reached for the paperweight. It didn't look like it would do much good as a weapon, but maybe she could use it as a distraction.

It took several more tries, but Cassie finally got the cuff off. She rubbed her bruised, raw wrist.

Martin gestured with the gun. "Head for the hallway. Both of you."

Cassie stumbled toward Addy. Although she didn't appear to be hurt physically, she was weak. Addy wrapped her arm around Cassie's waist and helped her to the door.

"To the right. We're going to the loading docks," Martin said.

They walked through the corridor, following Martin's directions, the overhead security lights illuminating the way.

Two oversize red doors loomed at the end of the hall. A sign affixed to the one on the right declared this the entrance to the factory floor. Another sign on the left cautioned that the area was for authorized personnel only and that protective gear must be worn at all times.

"Go on," Martin prodded.

Addy held on to Cassie with one hand and pushed the metal bar in the middle of the door with the other.

The space on the other side of the doors was dark.

Martin was obviously familiar with the space. He reached for the wall to their left, the dim light that trickled in from the door he still held open illuminating a panel of light switches on the wall.

Martin flicked each of the switches in turn, but nothing happened. The room remained shrouded in darkness.

It was now or never. Addy launched the paperweight toward the far end of the factory floor. The distraction worked as she'd hoped. Martin turned with the gun toward the sound of the glass breaking. Grabbing Cassie by the shirt, Addy half pulled, half dragged her behind an enormous machine to the right of the door and along an aisle of equipment.

She had no idea where they were going or if there was another exit from the factory floor.

She could hear Martin swearing at her and Cassie and at the lights that he still struggled to get on.

She reached into her purse, wrapping her

hand around her gun and unclipping it from its holster.

Addy didn't know whether to wish for the lights to come on or remain off. As much as the darkness hampered their advance to freedom, it also made it that much more difficult for Martin to find them.

"Are you familiar with the layout of this place?" Addy asked quietly, still half dragging her sister.

"No," Cassie whispered, wincing. "I've never been here before."

Cassie cradled her arm, and although Addy couldn't see an injury there, she knew firsthand that didn't mean there was none. The wound on her torso stretched and stabbed with pain.

They kept moving around large pieces of equipment and turned a corner.

Martin, wherever he was now, had gone ominously quiet.

They'd made it to the far wall of the large space when the harsh fluorescent overhead lights sprang on.

Addy pulled Cassie down behind a nearby machine and peered around it.

She didn't see Martin or any doors that might lead to safety, but she did spy a red-and-white exit sign hanging from the ceiling. Unfortunately, it was on the opposite side of the factory.

To make it to that side, she and Cassie would have to cross an area of the factory that offered no machines to hide behind.

As she considered how they could make it across the open area, Martin stepped into it, blocking the path to the exit.

"This is a waste of time, you know. Better to go quietly, gracefully, than to engage in this battle you cannot win," Martin shouted.

His eyes roamed over the space. He didn't know where they were, but that could change at any moment.

Addy looked at Cassie. She'd sunk to the floor, her back to the machine they hid behind, her breathing labored.

Rage tore through Addy. She had no idea what Cassie had been through in the past several days, but she'd survived.

Addy would be damned before they'd give up now.

She helped Cassie to her feet, taking most of her sister's weight.

If they could just get to that door, maybe even get out of it without Martin noticing...

They picked their way around the machines, using Martin's increasingly unhinged taunts as a guide to areas to avoid.

They'd made it to the point where they'd have

to cross the space that provided no cover when Martin fell ominously quiet.

Addy's heart rate kicked into warp speed. Was he setting them up? Watching and waiting until they stepped out into the open, giving him a clear shot at them?

Addy reached for the front of her shirt, but several things seemed to happen in that instant.

Cassie's legs gave out, sending the full weight of her body into Addy. Addy wrapped her free hand around her sister's waist, keeping her off the floor.

At the same moment, the door to the factory that Martin had used to lead her and Cassie onto the factory floor burst open. Shawn and Ryan swept in. Any relief Addy felt at seeing them was short-lived.

She sensed more than saw Martin step out from behind the machine to their left.

He grabbed Cassie by the hair, yanking her from Addy's unstable grip with enough force to make Cassie cry out and Addy stumble to the side.

Addy turned and faced the man who now held a gun to her sister's head. Out of the corner of her eye, she could see Shawn and Ryan advancing toward them quickly.

"Back up!" Martin's gun hand shook. "Back up now, or she's dead."

Shawn and Ryan stopped, but their guns remained pointed at Martin.

It might have been fear or adrenaline, but Cassie's wide eyes were more alert than they'd been since Addy had found her handcuffed to the filing cabinet. Hopefully, that rally would last long enough for all of them to get out of this with their lives.

Martin trained his wild gaze on Shawn and Ryan, giving Addy cover to slip her hand into her open purse unobserved.

"This isn't going to go your way, Raupp. Drop your weapon," Shawn said.

They stood in a lopsided triangle of sorts, Shawn and Ryan at one end and Addy at the other. Raupp and Cassie formed the tip at the top of the triangle.

"You're in no position to give orders. Drop your weapons or this pretty little thing's brains are going to be all over the floor."

Cassie flinched as Martin's grip on her hair tightened.

All the air fled Addy's lungs. Killing Cassie made no sense, but Raupp had rolled right on past rational a while ago. His scheme was all but over, and he was on his way to prison for a very long time. He had nothing to lose.

Addy kept her eyes locked on Cassie's face,

but out of the side of her eye she saw Shawn and Ryan share a glance.

Do it! Please do it! This could be just the distraction she needed.

As if he'd heard her telepathy, Shawn said, "Okay."

They both held out their guns and began slowly lowering them to the ground.

Addy's gaze never left Cassie's face. Shawn and Ryan weren't the only siblings communicating without words. As they slowly lowered their weapons, Cassie nodded slightly and wrenched away from Martin. She threw herself to the side with enough force that Martin was left with a clump of hair in his hand as Cassie fell to the floor.

Addy didn't hesitate. She pulled her gun from her purse and fired a single shot.

Martin jerked, his face registering a moment of surprise. He looked down at the blood spreading across his chest, letting his gun fall from his hand.

Ryan rushed toward Martin.

All Addy could see was Cassie. "Cassie!" She rushed to her sister's side, making it there at the same time Shawn did.

"Are you two okay?" Shawn's eyes never left Addy's face, though he'd directed the question at both of them.

Addy nodded. "He didn't hurt me, but we need to get Cassie medical help now."

Shawn gave her one more long look, assuring himself she knew that she was okay before pulling out his cell phone and stepping away.

"I'm fine," Cassie said, but the weakness of her voice belied the comment. Tears spilled over Cassie's cheeks. "I knew you'd find me."

Addy pulled her sister into an embrace. The sisters held on to each other for several seconds before Cassie spoke again. "Did you kill him?"

Addy looked over her shoulder.

Ryan had ripped off the bottom of Martin's dress shirt and was pressing it against his wound. Shawn held his cell phone to his ear, requesting police and medical assistance.

"I think he's still alive," Addy said, turning back to her sister.

Addy sent up a quick prayer. Even after everything he'd done, she didn't want Martin dead. Didn't want any man's death at her hands.

Shawn returned, crouching beside Addy. "Donovan and medics are on the way."

Addy raised her palm to his jaw and stroked the stubble blooming there. "Thank you."

He leaned into her touch. "For what?" Shawn smiled. "Once again your shooting saved the day, sweetheart."

Chapter Twenty-One

Cassie sat up in the hospital bed, a huge smile on her face. She had a presence. Shawn watched the corners of Gideon's mouth turn up a fraction, a rare phenomenon. The young woman had to have some kind of magical powers.

Shawn felt a light touch against his arm and looked into Addy's brown eyes as she came to a stop next to him just inside the hospital room door.

"Dr. Rose says she'll be fine in a day or two." Addy frowned. "At least physically. He suggested I find her someone to talk to about the whole ordeal."

Martin and Teddy hadn't physically hurt her, but psychological damage had the potential to be even more devastating.

"Therapy might not be such a bad idea. For Cassie or for you," Shawn said pointedly. Addy had gone through a trauma of her own—nothing close to what Cassie had suffered, but a trauma, nonetheless. He'd held her in the hour after Cassie had been brought into the hospital while she'd cried out the fear she'd been holding inside for nearly two weeks.

"Maybe." Addy moved her gaze from his face to her sister. "Maybe Cassie and I could go together."

Shawn put his arm around Addy's shoulder, pulling her in tightly against his side. Where she should be.

At least as far as he was concerned.

They'd both confessed to having feelings for each other, but they hadn't exactly had time to discuss what that meant for either of them.

He knew what it meant for him. He wanted a future with Addy, but he knew she wasn't positive she could achieve her professional goals and maintain a relationship. He didn't think she needed to choose, but would she come to the same conclusion?

Someone cleared their throat.

Shawn and Addy turned in tandem to find Donovan behind them. "I came to see if Miss Williams is up for giving her statement now."

Shawn, Addy, Gideon and Ryan had given their statements at the scene, but the EMTs had taken Cassie off to the hospital before she could give Donovan a complete statement. She had made it clear that Martin Raupp and Teddy Arbury had held her hostage for the last twelve days and that she suspected her ex-boyfriend Ben had been in on her kidnapping. Martin had also had her sign the phony resignation letter. She'd still have to flesh out some details for Donovan and testify if there was a trial, but Raupp would likely spend the rest of his life in jail.

Shawn felt Addy's body tense, and he was sure she was seconds from telling Donovan off. She still hadn't forgiven the man for taking such a hands-off approach to Cassie going missing.

"I'm fine to give my statement now, Sheriff." Cassie spoke up.

Addy shot Donovan a dark look but stood aside so he could enter the room and go to Cassie's bedside.

"If you don't mind, Miss Williams, it may be easier to do this in private." Donovan's eyes roamed over each of the men in the room and Addy before settling back on Cassie.

"I want my sister and Shawn to stay."

Donovan frowned but nodded his acceptance.

"I'll be in the waiting room," Ryan said.

Donovan retrieved a notebook from his

breast pocket and flipped to a clean page. "Why don't you start from the beginning and lay the whole thing out for me in your own time and way."

Shawn and Addy had been able to deduce some of the pieces regarding what had gone down with Spectrum and the falsified chips, but the details about Cassie's kidnapping remained fuzzy. Shawn was as interested as Donovan in finding out exactly why and how Cassie had ended up in the middle of a million-dollar fraud.

Cassie let out a deep breath. "I really don't know where to start, Sheriff. At first, the internship at Spectrum was great. The people were nice. I was learning a ton, just like I'd hoped when I delayed starting school and work." Cassie looked to Addy, almost in confirmation that this was the goal.

Addy smiled and nodded her agreement.

"As an intern, I did most of the filing. You know, the grunt work no one else wants to do, so they save for the lowest woman on the totem pole." Cassie grinned.

"I'm familiar with the practice." Donovan returned Cassie's grin.

"Anyway, after a while, I noticed some discrepancies between what was on the written inventory forms that came from the factory floor, the number that was in the computer and how many chips appeared to be coming off the assembly lines on the days I worked at the factory."

Donovan scribbled notes on his pad while Shawn and Addy listened with rapt attention.

"I'd been dating Ben for six weeks or so by this time, so I brought it up to him." Cassie frowned. "He got really nervous. Said I didn't know what I was talking about and blew me off." Her frown deepened. "I was already realizing he was kind of a jerk, and I was ready to break it off with him, anyway. Two days later, he came to my place uninvited. He'd been drinking a lot, from the smell of him. That was the last straw. I broke up with him, and he lost it. He went off on how I thought I was better than him and smarter than everyone, but he was the smart one. He said he was going to be rich soon, and I'd come crawling back."

"You should have called the sheriff," Addy said, rage dancing across her face.

Donovan nodded in agreement.

Cassie shook her head, looking down at her hands in her lap. "I thought it was the alcohol talking. I'd have thrown him out, but I didn't want him driving. He eventually wore himself out, and I told him he could sleep it off on the couch. He tripped over the leg of the coffee table, and a computer chip fell out of his pocket. I knew right away something was wrong. It had an Intellus logo on it. I picked it up before he could get to it, and everything kind of fell into place in my brain, you know."

Cassie looked from Shawn to Addy to Donovan.

Donovan blinked several times, his face a blank. "I'm sorry, I don't know anything about computers, except they don't like me and I don't like them. Can you spell it out for me?"

Cassie smiled at Donovan, and Shawn could have sworn he blushed a little. Addy's little sister was a charmer, even when she wasn't trying to be.

Then again, no one could be more charming in his book than the eldest Miss Williams.

"Tons of products, from your phone to your watch to any number of everyday household appliances, have at least one kind of computer chip in them," Cassie said, visibly warming up to the subject. "The manufacturers of these items don't make the chips themselves. They purchase them from companies like Spectrum and Intellus. Now imagine one in every five or ten or even a hundred products starts consistently failing because of the chip inside? As a manufacturer, that impacts your company reputation, and you're going to find another chip supplier."

"Like Spectrum if you've found that Intellus's chips are faulty." Donovan nodded, his pen tapping the notebook in his hand.

"Chip fraud is the fastest-growing form of fraud in the world right now." Cassie leaned her head back against the pillows.

"To the tune of billions worldwide." Shawn jumped into the conversation. "By selling faulty chips with Intellus's logo, Raupp was not only pocketing a small fortune, he also almost decimated the reputation of his competition."

"Okay, I think I understand. Let's go back a bit. What happened after you picked up the chip Ben dropped?" Donovan focused on Cassie again.

Cassie's forehead scrunched. "I don't remember exactly. I think I told him I was going to go to you, Sheriff. He must have hit me with something, because I felt a pain in the back of my head, and when I woke up I was in this little room. I didn't know where at first, but later I realized it was a panic room."

Donovan nodded. "We found a panic room in the basement of Martin Raupp's mansion. We're processing the house now."

"Mr. Raupp or that guy Teddy brought me food once or twice a day, but otherwise they left me there. I think the food was drugged. I tried to eat as little as possible because I was always so sleepy after eating."

Donovan slid a sidelong glance at Shawn. "We've arrested Mr. Arbury."

When Shawn had called Donovan to let him know they believed Martin Raupp was involved in Cassie's kidnapping and that they were on their way to the Spectrum factory where they believed he was holding her, he'd also told Donovan where he could find Teddy Arbury.

"Two days ago you called your sister?"

"The bathroom in the panic room flooded a few days before. The smell was awful." Cassie's nose crinkled, and her face twisted in disgust. "On the second day, I woke up after lunch, my hands tied behind my back, in an office. They'd moved me so they could have the bathroom fixed."

"How did you get a phone? And why didn't you call 911?" Donovan asked.

"If there was a phone in the room to begin with, they'd taken it out, but I was able to work one of the desk drawers open, and I found my wallet and cell phone inside. I used the facial recognition to unlock it and voice commands to call Addy, but I was still groggy from whatever they'd put in the food. Mr. Raupp must have heard me talking."

Donovan scratched the back of his neck and shifted his weight uncomfortably. "I'm sorry, but there is no good way to ask this next question, Miss Williams."

Addy's back straightened under Shawn's arm. She squeezed Cassie's hand in support.

"Why do you think Martin Raupp kidnapped you instead of, well, instead of—"

"Killing me?" Cassie visibly swallowed.

"Well, yes, ma'am."

The fire that ignited in Cassie when she'd begun talking seemed to have fizzled. "I don't know."

Shawn spoke up. "This is just speculation, but we think Raupp knew Intellus was onto the fraud. They weren't sure exactly who was behind it, which is why they hired us, but we were closing in. The death of a Spectrum intern would have invited scrutiny that Raupp probably wanted to avoid until after he'd put the fraudulent chips out into the market."

Donovan shook his head. "That makes sense. We may never get a for-sure answer. Neither Raupp nor Teddy is talking." Donovan closed his notebook. "It's hard to imagine something like this happening in my town." Donovan patted Cassie's knee. "I think that's all I need for now. You get well," he said before leaving the hospital room.

"Did Dr. Rose answer all your questions?" Cassie rolled her eyes at her sister.

Addy reached for Cassie's hand and gave it a squeeze. "Yes, he did. He wants to keep you for observation overnight, but he said you can go home tomorrow morning."

"Yippee. I am so ready for home. New York home."

"And I'm so ready to have you back home in New York." Addy smiled at Cassie.

"Shawn." Ryan's voice came from the doorway.

"Be right back." He planted a kiss on Addy's temple and earned a cheeky eyebrow raise from Cassie before exiting the room.

He and Shawn moved farther down the hall away from the door. From the hard set of Ryan's jaw, he wasn't going to like whatever his brother was about to say.

"Intellus wants a debrief ASAP. In person. We can be on a flight out in three hours if we leave now."

Shawn's head was shaking before Ryan finished his last sentence. "I can't leave Addy right now."

Ryan crossed his arms over his chest. "Addy and her sister are fine. Didn't I hear her say they were headed back to New York tomorrow?" When Shawn didn't reply, Ryan added,

Intellus is our client. You were the principal on this. No one else is going to be able to debrief as well as you."

"Go."

Shawn turned at the sound of Addy's voice behind him. Shawn shook his head. "I'm not going to leave you to deal with everything on your own."

Addy's shoulders rose, then dropped. "What everything? Cassie and I can get ourselves back to New York."

"I don't think—" He stopped when Addy stepped in close to him, wrapping her arms around his waist and looking up into his eyes.

"Go. I'll be here when you get back."

He placed a light kiss on Addy's lips. "Promise?"

Addy's smile was blinding. "Absolutely."

Chapter Twenty-Two

Dr. Rose discharged Cassie from the hospital at eight the next morning. They didn't even bother to stop at the sheriff's office and pick up the things Addy and Shawn had found in Cassie's attic. By eleven they were back in New York City.

Addy felt like it was the first time she'd taken a breath since Cassie went missing.

For three days after they got home, her entire focus was on taking care of Cassie. Her independent sister let her hover for two days, but her patience with the mothering had worn thin.

Cassie was out now, at a friend's house, working on getting some sense of normalcy back. Addy had received several recommendations for therapists. She and Cassie agreed that seeing one together could go a long way to helping them both heal. They had their first appointment next week.

On the second night they were back in New

York, they'd gone out for a nice dinner and had a long talk about the future. Cassie admitted she planned to turn down MIT's acceptance and attend university in the city. Addy couldn't be happier to keep her sister close, and considering Addy was now unemployed, she appreciated that Cassie's decision to attend school in the city took a lot of the financial pressure off.

Now here she was, less than a week before Christmas, sitting at the small desk in the corner of her bedroom, ostensibly to put out feelers, hoping to set up some job interviews in the new year. But she'd spent more time thinking about Shawn than searching job sites. They'd shared several short text conversations and two even shorter phone calls since he'd left the hospital headed for Silicon Valley. She missed him more than she could have imagined. In the few short days they'd spent together searching for Cassie, she'd fallen totally and irreversibly in love with Shawn West, despite her best efforts.

During their conversation last night, Shawn had told her that he might need to stay in California for another week.

The separation disappointed her, but it was the distant tone in his voice that scared her. She couldn't help but wonder if, now that the adrenaline had worn off, Shawn was reconsidering a relationship with her.

She inhaled deeply, let it out slowly and focused on the computer in front of her. She'd put out feelers and had received a surprising invitation to discuss a job opportunity from Brandon West, Shawn's brother.

Brandon West's firm was small, just him and a couple of paralegals, based on his website. But the work they did was innovative. They were a long way from offer and acceptance, but joining his firm would mean reimagining what her career could be. She wasn't sure if she was ready for that, so she hadn't responded to his email yet. The description of his firm and the work he did was intriguing, but she wasn't sure how she felt about working with Shawn's brother. Especially if she and Shawn didn't work out.

The doorbell rang.

She opened the door and froze.

Shawn stood in front of her.

"Hi." He smiled, but it was shaky and unsure. Very un-Shawn-like.

Her heart fell into her stomach, but she forced a smile onto her face. If he was there to call things off, she'd accept his decision with grace.

"Hi." The word came out thinner, breathier than she intended.

They stared at each other for a long moment before Shawn spoke. "May I come in?"

"Oh, yes, of course," she said, moving aside so he could stride past her into the apartment.

"What are you doing here?" she asked, closing the door and leading Shawn into the living room.

"I just followed one of your neighbors in. He didn't even look at me."

"That's not what I meant. You said you needed to be in California for another week."

"I know, but right after we got off the phone, I realized that the place I truly needed to be was with you."

"Really?" A smile so wide it hurt Addy's cheeks spread across her face.

Shawn's smile mirrored her own. "I think I knew it six months ago, when I caught you undressing me with your eyes across the reception hall at my brother's wedding."

She scoffed, but her smile didn't dim. "I was not undressing you with my eyes."

Shawn arched an eyebrow, his eyes blazing with heat. "Well, maybe you can do that later, then?"

A laugh bubbled out of Addy. "So I guess we're giving this relationship thing a whirl, then."

"For as long as we both shall live, princess. For as long as we both shall live."

* * * * *

Get 4 FREE REWARDS!

We'll send you 2 FREE Books plus 2 FREE Mystery Gifts.

Harlequin Romantic Suspense books are heart-racing page-turners with unexpected plot twists and irresistible chemistry that will keep you guessing to the very end.

FREE Value Over **$20**

YES! Please send me 2 FREE Harlequin Romantic Suspense novels and my 2 FREE gifts (gifts are worth about $10 retail). After receiving them, if I don't wish to receive any more books, I can return the shipping statement marked "cancel." If I don't cancel, I will receive 4 brand-new novels every month and be billed just $4.99 per book in the U.S. or $5.74 per book in Canada. That's a savings of at least 13% off the cover price! It's quite a bargain! Shipping and handling is just 50¢ per book in the U.S. and $1.25 per book in Canada.* I understand that accepting the 2 free books and gifts places me under no obligation to buy anything. I can always return a shipment and cancel at any time. The free books and gifts are mine to keep no matter what I decide.

240/340 HDN GNMZ

Name (please print)

Address   Apt. #

City   State/Province   Zip/Postal Code

Email: Please check this box ☐ if you would like to receive newsletters and promotional emails from Harlequin Enterprises ULC and its affiliates. You can unsubscribe anytime.

Mail to the **Harlequin Reader Service:**
IN U.S.A.: P.O. Box 1341, Buffalo, NY 14240-8531
IN CANADA: P.O. Box 603, Fort Erie, Ontario L2A 5X3

Want to try 2 free books from another series! Call 1-800-873-8635 or visit www.ReaderService.com.

Get 4 FREE REWARDS!

We'll send you 2 FREE Books plus 2 FREE Mystery Gifts.

PRESENTS

Off-Limits to the Crown Prince

KALI ANTHONY

PRESENTS

The Flaw in His Red-Hot Revenge

ABBY GREEN

Harlequin Presents books feature the glamorous lives of royals and billionaires in a world of exotic locations, where passion knows no bounds.

FREE Value Over $20

YES! Please send me 2 FREE Harlequin Presents novels and my 2 FREE gifts (gifts are worth about $10 retail). After receiving them, if I don't wish to receive any more books, I can return the shipping statement marked "cancel." If I don't cancel, I will receive 6 brand-new novels every month and be billed just $4.55 each for the regular-print edition or $5.80 each for the larger-print edition in the U.S., or $5.49 each for the regular-print edition or $5.99 each for the larger-print edition in Canada. That's a savings of at least 11% off the cover price! It's quite a bargain! Shipping and handling is just 50¢ per book in the U.S. and $1.25 per book in Canada.* I understand that accepting the 2 free books and gifts places me under no obligation to buy anything. I can always return a shipment and cancel at any time. The free books and gifts are mine to keep no matter what I decide.

Choose one: ☐ **Harlequin Presents Regular-Print** (106/306 HDN GNWY)   ☐ **Harlequin Presents Larger-Print** (176/376 HDN GNWY)

Name (please print)

Address   Apt. #

City   State/Province   Zip/Postal Code

Email: Please check this box ☐ if you would like to receive newsletters and promotional emails from Harlequin Enterprises ULC and its affiliates. You can unsubscribe anytime.

Mail to the **Harlequin Reader Service:**
IN U.S.A.: P.O. Box 1341, Buffalo, NY 14240-8531
IN CANADA: P.O. Box 603, Fort Erie, Ontario L2A 5X3

Want to try 2 free books from another series! Call 1-800-873-8635 or visit www.ReaderService.com.

*Terms and prices subject to change without notice. Prices do not include sales taxes, which will be charged (if applicable) based on your state or country of residence. Canadian residents will be charged applicable taxes. Offer not valid in Quebec. This offer is limited to one order per household. Books received may not be as shown. Not valid for current subscribers to Harlequin Presents books. All orders subject to approval. Credit or debit balances in a customer's account(s) may be offset by any other outstanding balance owed by or to the customer. Please allow 4 to 6 weeks for delivery. Offer available while quantities last.

Your Privacy—Your information is being collected by Harlequin Enterprises ULC, operating as Harlequin Reader Service. For a complete summary of the information we collect, how we use this information and to whom it is disclosed, please visit our privacy notice located at corporate.harlequin.com/privacy-notice. From time to time we may also exchange your personal information with reputable third parties. If you wish to opt out of this sharing of your personal information, please visit readerservice.com/consumerschoice or call 1-800-873-8635. **Notice to California Residents**—Under California law, you have specific rights to control and access your data. For more information on these rights and how to exercise them, visit corporate.harlequin.com/california-privacy.

HP21R2